Confectionately Yours

Save the Cupcake!

Lisa Papademetriou

SCHOLASTIC INC.

New York   Toronto   London   Auckland
Sydney   Mexico City   New Delhi   Hong Kong

All activities in this book should be performed with adult supervision. The publisher and author disclaim all liability for any accidents or injuries or loss that may occur as a result of the use or misuse of the information and guidance given in this book.

ISBN 978-0-545-22228-0

12 11 10 9 8 7 6 5 4 3 2 1   12 13 14 15 16 17/0

Printed in the U.S.A.   40

First printing, May 2012

Book design by Yaffa Jaskoll

To Zoë Papademetriou

Confectionately Yours

Save the Cupcake!

Freaking Out

I'm not usually the kind of girl who gets punched in the face. I guess this was just my lucky day.

"Hayley! Hayley, are you okay?" Marco's thick, straight eyebrows are pulled together. He reaches for my hand, but Artie pushes him away.

"What is *wrong* with you?" she shouts at him.

"I'm fine," I say from my place on the ground, but nobody hears me. Everyone is shouting and pointing fingers, and Marco is looking at me, his dark brown eyes brimming. I wish I could give him a hug. His fist in my face was an accident. Marco is one of my best friends — he would never hurt me on purpose. I know he must be feeling worse than I am right now.

I rub my jaw where his knuckles knocked against me and stand up so that everyone can see I'm okay. Marco was actually reaching for Ezra, but I got in between them. This is what I get for trying to stop a shoving match at a soccer game.

I don't even *like* soccer. Why did I have to get involved?

"Everybody step back," the coach commands. The players, referee, and miscellaneous people (me and Artie) mill around, everyone wandering slowly back to where they are supposed to be.

I look up at the blue sky. The game had started out well. I'd even been enjoying it for a while.

That alone probably should have made me suspicious.

It was a perfect day for a soccer game — sunny, with a cool breeze that kept it from getting too hot. I'd brought cupcakes that we could all share afterward. Artie and I sat in the first row of bleachers. As usual, she was patiently answering my questions about what was going on. I never understand what's happening when I watch soccer; I have some kind of sports deficiency. When I look out at the field, all I see is people in matching outfits running around like the fate of the world hangs on their ability to kick something. It's like *Attack of the Clones*, with a ball.

But it's important to Marco, and Artie plays, too, so I try to show up and cheer at their games. (Sometimes I cheer at the wrong moments, but it's the thought that counts.)

Everything had been going just fine until Marco shoved

Ezra, then Ezra shouted at him, and I rushed forward to help at the same moment that everyone on the field did the same thing.

"Hayley, I'm sorry!" Marco shouts as the coach starts to drag him toward the locker room.

"It was an accident!" I call after him, but I'm not sure he's even heard me. I desperately want to go after him, but I think I've "helped" enough for one day, and don't dare.

The zebra-striped referee has now ordered the teams back to the field. Artie and I retreat to the aluminum bleachers, where parents and other students stare at me for a moment, then return to their seats. The referee blows the whistle to restart the game.

"I can't believe Marco got into a fight with someone from *our own* team," Artie snaps, her eyes on the players.

"Ezra said something to him." I open and close my jaw, testing for damage, but there doesn't seem to be any. I don't think I'll even have a bruise. I only fell on the ground because I tripped over Ezra's feet when I was trying to grab hold of Marco's shoulder.

Ezra has white-blond hair, which makes him easy to spot among the clones. I glare at him as he races toward the opposing team's goal. I've never liked Ezra much, and I like him even less now. "Someone should have dragged him off the field, too."

"They don't drag you away for saying things; they drag you away for shoving," Artie shoots back. "Marco has to control his temper. He can't keep losing it!"

"The last time was two years ago."

"And it was just like this — he went ballistic and shoved Guy for no reason!"

"Maybe there was a reason."

Artie's hazel eyes lock on mine. "What good reason could there possibly be?"

I shrug, biting my lip.

My best friend heaves a sigh. She looks over at the gymnasium, where Marco is — no doubt — being lectured to within an inch of his life. "He's so sweet," she says slowly. "But he just gets so . . . mad sometimes."

"I know."

We stare out at the field for a while. I reach for the Tupperware box of cupcakes at my feet. We each take one, and nibble in silence as we watch the purple-suited players race around, trying to score.

Neither one of us feels like cheering anymore, I guess.

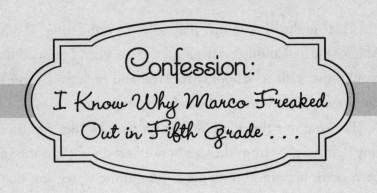

Confession:
I Know Why Marco Freaked
Out in Fifth Grade...

. . . And Artie doesn't. Nobody knows but me. That's because Marco made me promise not to tell.

After Marco screamed at Guy Poole and shoved him so hard that he knocked over a desk, Marco was suspended for two days. His father, red-faced and frowning, had to come to school and pick him up.

I didn't see him when I got home from school, and I didn't see him the next day, either. Artie was unusually talkative on our walks, almost as if she was trying to drown Marco's absence in words.

During one of her brief silences, I said, "I wonder what Marco is doing right now."

She heard me, all right, but she just squinted up at the clouds, and then started describing Jennifer Winston's awful new shoes.

That night, I couldn't fall asleep, wondering about Marco. He had another day of suspension, then I guessed he would just walk to school with Artie and me again. Artie's house was behind mine. Marco lived next door.

Looking out the window, I saw a flash — like a bolt of tiny lightning — from the tree house next door. I must have been tired, because it took me a full minute to register that the light must be from a flashlight.

It could be Sarah, I thought. But Marco's sister hardly ever used the tree house. It was Marco's place.

I don't know what made me do it, but I got out of bed and slipped my feet into a pair of sneakers. My room was on the ground floor, at the back of the house, and in the corner it had a door to the outside, plus a set of concrete stairs. I moved a pile of stuffed animals away from the door and walked out, careful to leave the door unlocked behind me.

I crossed the lawn and walked over to the tree. It was strange and thrilling to be out under the thumbnail moon. I climbed up three rungs of the ladder and whispered, "Marco."

Quiet.

"Marco," I whispered. "It's Hayley."

A pale face peeked out through the window. He didn't speak, just placed a finger to his lips and motioned for me to come up, so I scaled the ladder and hauled myself in through the crude door frame.

Marco stood up when he saw me. He had been sitting in a corner, reading comics. The flashlight was lying on top of one of the pages, illuminating one of the X-Men in fine detail, then fading into the darkness.

"Hi," I said.

"Hi."

"What are you doing out here?"

Marco shrugged. "I just had to get out of my room. I've been stuck in there for a day and a half."

"What?"

Marco turned away from me, fumbled with the flashlight, and turned it off. "I'm grounded. Like, in solitary confinement. Mom brings my meals, and I'm allowed out to do one hour of yard work a day." He laughed bitterly. "Dad says physical exercise is important."

I didn't know what to say. "I'm sorry."

"I'm not." In the darkness, his words were flinty, as if they could strike sparks.

"You're not?"

"Guy Poole is a —" He paused, trying to think of something that was bad enough.

"What did he do?"

Marco hesitated a moment. Finally, he spat it out. "He put some tacks on Kyle Kempner's seat."

"Seriously?" Kyle Kempner was in our class, and I'd always thought he was a sweet guy because he was totally nice to me even though I made an idiot out of myself the first time I met him in fourth grade. It was the first day of school, and I was wearing a denim skirt and a vintage bowling shirt with the name *Fred* stitched over the pocket. So I saw this curly-haired, smiley guy talking to my friend Annie, and I walked up and said hello. Annie introduced us, and I said, "My name is Hayley, but you can call me Fred."

"Fred?" Kyle smiled, as if he suspected that there was a joke that he was missing.

"Yeah, Fred." I gestured to my shirt.

He shook his head. "I don't get it."

This is when Annie dove in. "Her shirt has the name Fred on it," she said, and I was totally confused. I was standing there for like five minutes wondering why this kid couldn't read, until Kyle's aide came over. He walked away, and Annie whispered, "He's blind," and I felt like the biggest loser on earth.

But Kyle never acted embarrassed, or like I was a jerk, or anything. In fact, whenever I said hi, he would say, "Hey, Fred!" and give me a huge smile. It turned out that he could see a little — large shapes, some colors — just not well. But he could recognize voices in an instant.

Anyway, I couldn't imagine why anyone would put tacks on his seat, unless they were . . . well, some kind of word from a cable show.

"Why would anyone do that to Kyle?" I repeated.

Marco didn't answer; he just went on with his story. "So I was the first one back from lunch, and I saw the tacks and grabbed them off the seat before Kyle could sit on them, and Guy tried to make me put them back. He said it would be hilarious — Kyle wouldn't even see it coming." His voice lowered a bit. "But I wouldn't do it."

"Why didn't you tell anyone?"

"Because I didn't want Kyle to know." The words were soft as a flutter from a moth wing.

"Oh, Marco." I put my hands to my face. "This is all wrong. And now you're suspended and locked in your room."

He shushed me, and we stood stock-still, listening in the darkness.

"Look, I've got to go," Marco said after a moment. "I just wanted to get out for a while. Promise me you won't tell anyone, okay? It's not that bad, really — I just read most of the time — and it's almost over. My sentence is done tomorrow at three."

"I promise." I reached for his hand, and his fingers touched mine. I wanted to say something, but I didn't know what. He squeezed my fingers and then disappeared by inches as he went down the ladder.

I sat in the tree house for a long time by myself, listening to the quiet of the neighborhood, broken only by the occasional car rolling by. After a while, I climbed down and walked back to my room. I closed the door softly and put my stuffed animals back in their places. As I climbed into my bed, I noticed that the hems of my pajama bottoms were wet with dew. I stared out at the moon, thinking about Kyle and Marco and Guy, and what it means to have a temper.

It's not always a bad thing.

Spicy Mexican Chocolate "Hotheads"
(makes approximately 12–15 cupcakes)

These cupcakes come with a little "surprise" in the center. A good surprise. Not like a peach pit, or something.

INGREDIENTS:
- 1 cup all-purpose flour
- 2 tablespoons cornstarch
- 1/2 cup cocoa powder, unsweetened
- 1 teaspoon baking powder
- 1/2 teaspoon baking soda
- 3/4 teaspoon salt
- 1 teaspoon ground cinnamon
- 1/8 teaspoon cayenne pepper
- 1 cup milk
- 1 cup sugar
- 1/3 cup canola oil
- 1 teaspoon vanilla extract
- 1 teaspoon almond extract

INSTRUCTIONS:

1. Preheat the oven to 350°F. Line a muffin pan with cupcake liners.

2. In a large bowl, sift together the flour, cornstarch, cocoa powder, baking powder, baking soda, salt, cinnamon, and cayenne pepper, and mix.

3. In a separate large bowl, mix together the milk, sugar, oil, vanilla extract, and almond extract, and whisk. Slowly add the dry ingredients to the wet, and beat with a whisk or handheld mixer until smooth.

4. Fill cupcake liners halfway full, then gently place a spicy ganache ball in the center of each cupcake, pressing it down a little, and top with a few tablespoons of batter so that the ganache ball ends up "inside" the cupcake. (See ganache recipe on the next page.) Bake for 22–25 minutes, then serve immediately, so the goodness inside is properly gooey.

Chocolate Ganache (for molten centers)
(makes approximately 2 cups)

INGREDIENTS:
- 10 ounces semisweet chocolate chips
- 1 cup heavy cream
- 1 tablespoon agave syrup or corn syrup
- 1 teaspoon vanilla extract
- 1/2 teaspoon cayenne pepper

INSTRUCTIONS:
1. Place the chocolate chips, cream, and agave or corn syrup into a microwave-safe bowl and heat for 45 seconds. Remove from microwave and stir. If the chips are not melted, heat again in 10-second increments, stirring each time, until fully melted.
2. Whisk in vanilla extract and cayenne pepper. Place in the refrigerator for 1–2 hours and allow to firm.
3. When firm, remove from the refrigerator and scoop balls of ganache, rolling them into the size of a walnut. Place balls on wax paper, and keep in the refrigerator until ready to use.

A Fit of Passion

"Oh, those fairy cakes look divine," my grandmother — we call her Gran — says as I spread thick, dark frosting across the smooth, brown dome of a still-warm cupcake. "Simply divine!" She smiles at me, and the wrinkles at the edges of her pale blue eyes crinkle. "That's a proper treat for high tea."

Gran is from England, and she's very into the idea of high tea. She keeps thinking it will catch on here, but I have to say that Northampton, Massachusetts, isn't exactly clamoring for clotted cream at four P.M. Still, people do come to the Tea Room, my grandmother's café. But I think that's mostly because Gran makes the best scones in the world. Seriously. The world.

"Should we set them in the display case?" Gran asks.

"Do you really think they look good enough?" I ask. I hadn't thought of selling the cupcakes. I'd just made them because I like to experiment with flavors and my grandmother's industrial mixer.

My grandmother cocks her head. "Right," she says. In a flash, she pulls out a sleeve of white frosting and replaces the tip. A moment later, she has drawn a single white heart at the top of the chocolate frosting. "Lovely," she pronounces, and gives me a wink. She takes a bite of the cupcake. "Well, that's surprising!" she says, nodding her approval. "Let's frost them all this way — a small decoration makes all the difference. Place them at the top of the left case, please." Then she bustles off to help a customer.

I get to work frosting more cupcakes, and the door bursts open with a jingle and an explosion of pink and purple flowers. A dark head peeks out from behind the flower arrangement, and Mr. Malik gives me a smile, nearly dazzling me with his white teeth. "What is smelling so delicious in here?"

"Oh, Mr. Malik, what have you brought for us this week?" my grandmother asks. Do you see how British she is? She's known Mr. Malik for eight years, and she still calls him "Mr. Malik." He's from Pakistan, so he's just as bad, calling her "Mrs. Wilson," even though my grandfather died before I was born.

"Mrs. Wilson, I have brought for you some alstroemeria, freesia, and a few orchids — all arranged by my own hands."

He bows his head slightly as he places the bouquet by the cash register.

Gran flashes him her twinkliest smile and reaches under the counter for an empty blue vase and a bag of scones. "And I have here some ginger-pear scones, made by *my* own hands," she says as she gives Mr. Malik the bag and the vase from last week's arrangement.

I've seen this ritual many times before — it happens every Thursday afternoon at 4:15, regular as the changing of the guard. I even know what Mr. Malik will say next: "Manna from heaven." And then my grandmother will say, "Will you join me for tea, Mr. Malik, and perhaps a madeleine?" And then Mr. Malik will say, "Yes."

They are like two peas in a pod. I have no idea how they ended up with shops beside each other on the same street in Western Massachusetts. It's enough to make you think about God and fate and luck and all kinds of deep stuff.

Except, this time, Mr. Malik doesn't say yes. Instead, he says, "Of course, Mrs. Wilson, but I think I might prefer one of these delectable-looking cupcakes in your granddaughter's hands."

I'm so surprised, I nearly drop my cupcake.

"Not a madeleine?" My grandmother is as shocked as I am.

"How can I resist the aroma?" Mr. Malik asks. "You don't mind, Hayley? You aren't keeping them?"

"I'm honored," I say, which is completely over-the-top, I guess, but also true. I place the cupcake on a white plate and hand it over.

He takes a bite. "Ah!" And he laughs, as if I have fooled him. "Sweet and fiery! You can't tell where one stops and the other begins."

"They're called Hotheads," I say. "Cocoa, cinnamon, and a little cayenne pepper."

"Just the thing to get the blood moving! We'll all be in a fit of passion later, I presume."

I blush a little, until I remember that "a fit of passion" is a British expression for getting angry.

My grandmother has a pot of Earl Grey all ready, and she and Mr. Malik bustle off to have their Thursday chat about politics. The only two people in Northampton who care about high tea.

I look down at the cupcake in my hand. Sweet and fiery. I suppose I was thinking of Marco when I made these, though I didn't realize it. That's him.

It's him exactly.

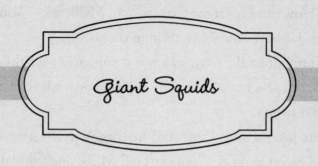

Giant Squids

Marco backs into the door, smooshing his backpack against the metal bar and forcing it wide open, then stands stiff as a soldier so Artie and I can walk through. "Thanks," I say, and he nods at me with this raised-eyebrow look that manages to say *You're welcome* and *Whatever* at the same time.

Marco had apologized again the minute he saw me at the bus stop. "I'm so sorry," he said. "Ezra just —"

"It's okay."

"Not really." Marco shrugged. "It's not really okay that I lose it sometimes."

Then he'd been quiet on the ride to school, which wasn't hard, given that Omar and Jamil had been rapping at the top of their lungs in the back row. We have a crazy bus that always manages to smell like sweaty feet, and it's usually a lot of fun. But earlier today — with Marco so quiet and Artie busy chatting with Alison Noel, an eighth grader I don't know — I'd been missing our quiet walks to and from the elementary school.

From third to fifth grade, Marco, Artie, and I walked together every single day. Back then, I would have had a chance to ask Marco what made him so mad, or else we would have been able to talk about something else that would have smoothed over the awkwardness.

Now we just give raised-eyebrow looks and move around each other in silence, like fish in a bowl.

"Hayley! Hey — Hayley!" A redhead with purple bangs rushes up to us, waving a pile of papers. She grins and announces, "I'm on a project."

"Hey, Meghan. What's up?"

"We're ditching the mascot," Meghan tells us.

"Who's *we*?" Marco asks. "Is this official class-rep business?"

Yes, this is our seventh-grade class rep — this girl, right here, wearing a headband with a pink sparkly flower on it, and a black-and-white tunic over a pair of black leggings. "Hopefully, official business. Seriously, we've been the Purple Pintos since 1974." She holds out her clipboard, and I notice that she has on blue sparkly nail polish.

"What's wrong with the Purple Pintos?" Marco asks.

Artie looks at him. "Are you serious?"

"No," Marco says.

"It's ridiculous, right?" Meghan shakes her head, her blue eyes wide. "You're on the soccer team. Do you want to go to another tournament with a purple horse on the van?"

A shadow falls over Marco's face at the mention of the soccer team, but he just says, "No, thanks."

"So what's it going to be?" I ask.

"I'm hoping for the Giant Squids," Meghan says. "You know, they can kill whales and they're dangerous and mysterious — only one has ever been photographed alive! Or I was thinking we could be something really rad — like, you know, Pi."

"Pie?" Marco asks. "Like, blueberry pie?"

"No — pi, like the mathematical constant. I just thought it would be different, you know? Like we're getting down to the essence of the universe."

I notice Artie rolling her eyes. Right. In addition to looking like she just got kicked out of an all-girl funk band, Meghan Markerson is a big science and math nerd.

"Pi is even worse than the Purple Pintos," Artie says.

"Really?" Meghan looks a little surprised, but seems to accept Artie's opinion. "Okay, then I'm for the Giant Squids. But, whatever, this petition isn't for either one of those things. It's just to get rid of the Purple Pintos. Then the whole school can vote on a new mascot."

"I kind of liked Blueberry Pie," I say. "Like, 'Come and get a piece of this.'"

Meghan laughs, and then holds out the petition again. "You'll get a chance to suggest it once we get rid of the Pintos," she says. "Just sign at the next space."

I pull a pen out of my bag.

"Are you seriously signing?" Artie asks.

I look at her a moment, her head cocked, her hazel eyes wide. "Why not?" I ask.

She just shrugs. When I'm finished, Meghan holds out the clipboard to Artie, but she shakes her head.

"I'll sign," Marco says.

"Thanks," Meghan says warmly when he hands the clipboard back to her. "Giant Squids, here we come!" She gives us a wink, then shouts out, "Jamil!" and runs after her next victim.

"We have a lunatic as class rep," Artie says, watching Meghan corner the lanky, dark-haired boy.

"At least she's doing something," Marco replies. "I've always hated that stupid mascot, but I never even thought of getting rid of it."

Artie looks at me, but I just press my lips together. This

isn't really something I feel strongly enough about to get into an argument either way.

"Come on, you guys. Meghan Markerson is nuts!" Artie hitches her messenger bag higher onto her shoulder. "Who even voted for her?"

"I guess the two Jameses split the vote," Marco says.

Philip and Scott James both ran for class rep against Meghan. They're both wildly popular, but they're identical twins, and I secretly think that lots of people aren't sure which one is which. If you put their votes together, they beat Meghan by a good margin. But individually, they were each fifteen votes shy of victory.

"I don't know if she's crazy," I say. "She just has her own ideas."

"She's so *loud*," Artie says, and that's that.

I'm not about to argue with her about it. We'll see.

Crazy is as crazy does, right?

Confession:
I Voted for Meghan Markerson

*W*ell, first off, I have to admit that I didn't really think she would *win*. I mean, the Jameses are popular. Way popular. What I didn't realize was that they are popular as a unit. The Twins. And the Twins weren't running. In fact, they were running *against* each other, which freaked some people out, to be perfectly honest. It didn't help that they both had campaign posters with their faces plastered on them. Eerie.

But that's not the real reason that I voted for Meghan.

I know that Artie has a point. Meghan can be loud and in-your-face. And a lot of people don't like the fact that she's always talking in class, answering questions or giving her opinion, like that we shouldn't study wars because it only encourages bad behavior in governments and low expectations in voters. I don't always agree with everything she says, but at least she's *interesting*. She doesn't wear the same thing that everyone else does, which right now, at our school, is skinny jeans and flats. And she doesn't look like everyone else, and she sure as heck doesn't think like everyone else.

I like those things about her, but that's not why I voted for her, either.

I voted for her because she helped me with my locker.

It was a week after my dad had moved out, a rainy Monday morning, and I was dripping all over the place, standing at my locker and twisting the built-in combination lock . . . but I couldn't remember the numbers. All I knew was that there was a seventeen in it. Somewhere.

And I was about to cry, but I didn't want anyone to know, so I just kept turning the knob, hoping the numbers would come to me.

Meghan's locker is three down from mine, and she pulled out her book and notebook, and clanged the door shut. She leaned against the bank of lockers and watched me for a minute, then said, "Blanking?"

I looked at her. She was hugging her notebook to her chest, and her eyes were kind.

"Yeah," I admitted.

"I'm lucky — my combination's so easy. Nineteen, twenty-three, twenty-nine."

"What's so easy about that?"

"Three prime numbers in a row!" Meghan smiled, like she'd drawn a winning lottery ticket. "Can you believe it?"

"Um."

We were silent for a moment, and I expected her to walk off, but she didn't. "You probably just have a lot on your mind," she said at last.

"Yeah." *And the Understatement of the Year Award goes to . . .*

"Are you okay?"

I thought it over. "Not really."

She waited, like she thought I might want to spill my guts to her. But I really didn't. I mean, I hardly knew her. She wasn't my best friend, or anything.

But Meghan didn't push me. She just put a hand on my arm. Then she said, "I know — I totally space out sometimes, too. Like, I have this stupid crazy crush on Ben Habib, and sometimes I just float off. . . ."

"Ben Habib?"

"I know. Dumb!"

"Why? He's cute — and nice."

"Eh! His parents are strict Muslims! He's not going to date some crazy Jewish girl like me. We're like Romeo and Juliet . . . except that he has no idea I'm alive." She sighed dramatically and put a hand to her forehead. Then she looked me dead in the eye. "If you tell anyone, I will kill you."

That made me laugh. "Okay. Promise." I smiled at her. "Oh!"

"You remembered it," she said.

"Yep." I turned the dial, and the locker popped open.

"Good job." And she walked off down the hall, her crazy fuchsia scarf trailing behind her.

So that was it. I voted for Meghan Markerson because she was the only person who noticed that I seemed down while my parents were splitting up.

Artie never asked me how I was. I tried to talk to her about it once, but she just changed the subject. I guess she couldn't handle hearing what it was like to have your dad move out. Not that I had any idea, anyway. What's it like? It's like . . . like feeling frightened all the time. Not knowing what to say to your parents, what might make them burst into tears. It's like realizing that they don't love you as much as you thought, that their own lives are more important to them than your life is.

It's just like that.

Artie didn't want to hear it. And Marco — that's a whole other story.

But Meghan actually seemed to care. At least she was willing to listen.

And she got my vote.

Drama at My Locker

"Artemis!" a tall guy with blond hair calls as Artie and I are yanking books and binders.

My heart stumbles a bit and I glance at Artie as she smiles and shouts, "Hey, Devon!"

"Do you know Devon McAllister?" I'm whispering, because he's actually walking toward us. It's a bit of a surprise, because he's a year above us, in eighth grade.

"Yeah," but she doesn't have time to explain before he props himself against the locker beside hers.

"Hey," he says warmly, smiling at her, and for a moment, my head is spinning. He has the most beautiful lips. It's embarrassing to say that, but it's true. Like, he should be a lip model, if that even exists. He could model ChapStick. And his eyes — they're blue, but not bright blue, more like slate blue, and serious.

I've been crazy about him since the first day of school last year. I was running to class and trying to shove two books into my backpack at the same time, and I ran smack into him in the hall. He reached for my dropped books at the same time I did, and we cracked our heads together.

He winced and rubbed his head while I picked up my books and mumbled that I was sorry. Then I ran off.

Wow, it's really romantic when I write it down like that.

Anyway, the point is that he is the kind of guy who would totally pick up your books for you. Unless you head-butted him, like I did.

And also, he's really good-looking. And did I mention he's an eighth grader?

So, naturally, I tried not to think about him. I had never mentioned my crush to anyone — not even Artie.

And here he is, standing one person away from me, on the other side of my best friend. I just might pass out and drop my books again.

"Callback list goes up on Friday," he says to Artie.

"I know; I'm so nervous."

"Don't be! You'll make it. Your cold reading was great."

"Really?" she asks.

I'm about to die. He's so sweet! And I know Artie is really grateful to hear this; she was so nervous about auditioning for the school musical that she nearly refused to try out. I had to drag her there. But she's got a great voice, and Artie doesn't seem to realize that she's totally gorgeous. She belongs onstage.

I'm leaning toward them now, nodding and smiling like I'm part of this conversation, but Devon doesn't look my way.

"Hey, did you hear about that guy who shoved Ezra at the soccer game?" he says out of the blue.

"Oh, yeah." Artie blushes. "That's Marco."

"You know him? Wasn't that weird?"

"Not if you know Marco."

"Really?"

I want to say something here, but nobody's actually talking to me, so I just lean back and sort through my books, pretending I'm really absorbed in putting them in alphabetical order and not just eavesdropping and thinking about Devon's lips.

Devon and Artie chat a little while longer, then his friends shout to him from across the hall and he says good-bye.

Once he's gone, Artie turns to me and smiles but she doesn't say anything.

"So . . ." I prompt.

"So." She pulls out another notebook and slams her locker shut.

"So — I didn't know you knew Devon."

"I don't. I mean, I just met him at the audition the other day."

"And?" I prompt again.

Artie shrugs. "He thinks I'll make the callback. I'm not so sure. He will, though. He was great."

"Well, would you mind introducing me next time he comes over?"

Artie turns to me, her mouth open. "Ohmigosh, Hayley! I'm so rude!"

"No big deal."

"I'm really sorry."

"Seriously, no big deal," I say, but I'm glad she feels a little bad. Artie can be a space case, and she's awful at introducing me to people.

"It's just — everyone knows Devon. I was wondering why you were being so quiet." Artie bites her lip.

This irks me. *Everyone knows Devon. She* didn't even know him until two days ago!

"Next time," Artie says with a smile.

"Sure," I say, hoping against hope that there actually will be a next time.

Sticky Stuff

"Need some help?" my mom asks as she slips into my room.

"What makes you ask?" A giant poster of Monet's *Water Lilies* peels off my wall and falls on my head. "Grr! Why doesn't this stupid sticky stuff ever stick?"

Mom laughs. "It's not straight, anyway." She kicks off her shoes and steps onto my twin bed. She holds up the poster, rubs the sticky stuff between her fingers, and replaces it on the back, then smashes it up against the wall. "You've got to *make* it stick," she says. "Straight now?"

I jump off the bed and sit down on Chloe's. "Looks good."

Mom smiles and plops down beside me, cross-legged. She looks young in her pink sweatshirt and jeans, even though she's kind of an older mom. She was thirty-five when she had me, thirty-nine when she had Chloe. Mom doesn't like me to tell people her age, but anyone who can add could figure it out. "How's the room working out?"

I shrug. "It's okay."

Mom looks around and sighs. The room is pretty disorganized. Chloe and I are still trying to figure out where everything goes. The biggest problem is that Chloe doesn't really care, but I don't want to make all the decisions by myself. So we have a pile of boxes in the corner.

I look at Mom sitting on my slightly rumpled, blue-and-white bedspread. We just repainted my room in the old house to match it last year — a beautiful pale blue like the edge of the sky on a hot day. But now some other kid is living in that room. Or maybe it's an office. And here I am, in a too-narrow room with dingy mauve paint and a falling-down poster.

"It's hard not having your own space."

"I don't mind." I'm not sure if this is true or not, but I decide to give it the benefit of the doubt.

Mom smiles at me. "It's just for a little while," she says.

"I know."

Silence pulses between us.

"Gran tells me that you've been helping at the café."

"She's selling my cupcakes. Mr. Malik bought one yesterday, and came in for another today."

"I heard. That's great." Mom smiles again, and this time it's a real smile that lights up her whole face. She leans forward and says, "Guess what — I have a job interview tomorrow."

"What? Awesome!"

"Now I just have to figure out what to wear."

"Black pants, red shirt."

She laughs. "You have it all figured out?"

"I've been planning," I admit.

Mom looks thoughtful, and I wonder if I've made her feel bad. I didn't mean to. It's just — Mom got laid off a couple of months ago. She used to be an office manager, and the office decided to downsize. That's why we moved in with Gran. Of course, Gran makes it sound like we moved in because she's some decrepit old lady who needs help running her tea shop, but I'm not sure if even Chloe is buying that one. Mom doesn't want to help run the tea shop. She doesn't even drink tea, and she can't bake a scone to save her life. We're here because we're out of money.

"Where's the interview?" I ask.

"At a doctors' office," she says. "A practice. Seven doctors."

"That'll be good." I just hope she gets it. She's only had two interviews so far, and neither one of them panned out. Mom unfolds her legs and steps off the bed.

"Come here, you," she says, pulling me into a hug. I hug back, trying not to feel desperate. She needs this job, and we both know it. The Tea Room isn't exactly a huge moneymaker.

Just then, Chloe bursts in through the door, her ponytail half-undone and scraggly. "Why is everyone on my bed?" she demands.

"Join us," Mom says.

Chloe smiles and hops onto the bed, and we all snuggle together for a minute. For a moment I'm reminded of three-year-old Chloe, who sang constantly and was a fountain of kisses and hugs.

"Can Horatio come over for dinner?" she asks suddenly.

"Horatio?" Mom repeats, obviously delighted. "He hasn't come to dinner in ages!"

"Is it okay?" Chloe asks.

"Of course," Mom says, giving my younger sister a squeeze. But I'm not so happy. I've never liked Horatio much, and I was pretty glad when he sort of disappeared for a while. But he's back, I guess.

I just hope he doesn't sit next to me.

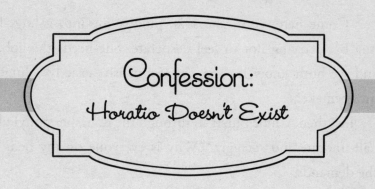

Confession:
Horatio Doesn't Exist

Seriously. He's my sister's imaginary friend. Yes, she is eight and still has an imaginary friend. Is that weird, or am I paranoid?

My mom thinks it's adorable, and Horatio's name brings up all sorts of nostalgia for her. He first appeared when Chloe was less than two years old, but we just called him *Boy* then. We would have tea parties with Boy, and celebrate his birthday, and take him sledding with us and stuff.

He wasn't named Horatio until she turned three. Mom says it was really weird — she has no idea how Chloe came up with the name. It's not like there was another kid in her day care named Horatio or something.

Anyway, Horatio and Chloe would play tag in the yard, or read together, or have long chats in the living room. It is very peculiar to watch your three-year-old sister play with

Duplos while having an intense conversation in a low voice with nobody. Like, it's the kind of thing that's always happening in horror movies, and I guess a part of me has been sort of waiting for one of her freaky stuffed animals to come alive, or for the walls to start bleeding, or something.

I guess that's part of why he gives me the creeps.

But the other part is my fear that Horatio is actually Chloe's best friend . . . and that makes me sad. She's always been shy, and ever since learning how to read, she spends most of her time by herself, sitting under a tree, face hidden behind a book. Shouldn't she have real friends? I mean — she's eight, not three. Mom doesn't seem worried about it, but I am.

I have to admit, I was hoping he was gone for good, but I'm not surprised that he's back. With everything that's happened to us in the past few months, I know Chloe needs a friend.

I guess I've just been wishing that she would find a real one.

From the Phone Files:
Part 1

"Hello?"

"Oh, you're not screening your calls?"

"Hi, Dad."

"I'm surprised you picked up the phone. You hardly ever do. Well, how are you?"

"Good."

"Just good?"

"Everything's good, Dad. Getting my room set up."

"So . . . what should we do this weekend?"

"I don't know. See a movie, maybe? Chloe wants to see that new one about the princess and the —"

"I don't want to just sit in the dark and not talk to you guys."

"Okay."

"I thought we could go apple picking."

"Okay."

"You don't sound excited about it. I thought you loved apple picking."

"I do — it's just . . . It sounds good."

"Chloe likes apple picking."

"Right, Dad. Right. I mean — do you know how to make applesauce?"

"What's that supposed to mean?"

"Nothing. I just — we usually go apple picking with Mom."

"Okay, Hayley. . . ." Dad sighs.

"But there's no reason we can't go with you, I guess. It'll be fun."

"You bet it will."

"Can I bring Artie?"

"No."

"Why not?"

"Because this is our time together, Hayley. If you bring Artemis, then Chloe will want to bring a friend. . . ."

"She can bring Horatio."

"Very funny. Look, I'll pick you up Saturday morning at nine. Sharp."

"Fine."

"You don't sound excited."

"I am. I'm . . . thrilled."

"Okay, Hayley, look — let me speak to Chloe."

"I don't know where she is right now."

"Well, go find her."

"Okay. Hold on a minute."

"See you Saturday."

"Yeah."

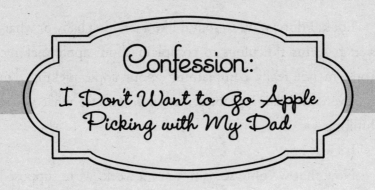

Confession:
I Don't Want to Go Apple Picking with My Dad

I.

Don't.

Want.

To.

Idon'twanttoIdon'twanttoIdon'twanttoIdon'twanttoIdon'wanttoIdon'twantto.

ot.tnaw.t'nod.I!

A Dot Tint Now

Dawn It Not To

Tad In Town To

Oh, who am I kidding? I'm going. Chloe is all excited — she wants me to bring Mom's recipe for apple cake. It's the one thing our mother knows how to bake. Chloe doesn't even seem to have thought about how painful that would be for Mom. Not that I'm going to explain it to Chloe. I'm not that mean.

Look, I don't want to sound like a jerk or a baby or whatever. It seems ridiculous to complain about apple picking. And I'm not really complaining about apple picking. I'm not even complaining about my dad, if that's what you're thinking.

It's just . . .

Now that we only see him once a week, we're supposed to Do Stuff together. But when he used to live with us, we never had to do anything. We could just hang out and make pancakes or read the newspaper or watch a Godzilla movie on TV. Dad never complained if I wanted to hang out with Artie or Marco, or anyone.

I didn't have to cram in all of this quality time with Dad. He was just there. Or else he was at work, and I didn't really think about him much. Now we have to Talk and Spend Time Together. Back then, we could just ignore each other or be together in quiet ways.

I guess it sounds bad to say that I miss having my dad live with us because I miss taking him for granted.

But that's the truth.

Horrible me.

The Chapter in Which I Finally Speak to Devon

The noise of people chatting and silverware clinking floats through the air on a cloud of fried-food smell. I look over at the salad bar, where Artie hovers, debating with her usual thoroughness the choice between garbanzo and kidney beans. Her parents are all earthy-crunchy, and whenever Artie brings food from home, it's something in the avocado-sandwich-on-homemade-seven-grain-bread family. My mom is more of a peanut-butter-and-jelly kind of mom. Today she packed a turkey sandwich, a slightly mashed pear, and a bag of chips.

"This is what I get for forgetting my lunch," Artie says as her plate clatters onto the orange table. A healthy salad gleams before her, beside a whole wheat roll and an apple.

"Looks pretty good," I say.

"They don't even have any sunflower seeds to go on the salad!" Artie complains, spearing a grape tomato.

"And they call this place a school cafeteria?" I shake my head.

"I just like it how I like it," Artie says.

"Yeah. I know the feeling." I look down at my own sad little half-squashed sandwich. "Mom always puts too much mayo on my sandwiches."

"Can't you tell her to stop?"

"I've tried, but she doesn't get it."

"Annoying, but what are you going to do about it? You'll just have to live with it."

"Yeah." I take a bite of my pear. "I guess I could pack my own lunch."

"There's an idea." Artie makes a face.

It's funny. I've never had this thought before. Isn't that weird? Like, packing lunch has always been part of Mom's job description. But why? Why not my dad? He makes good sandwiches. Even *I'm* a way better cook than she is — why shouldn't I pack my own lunch? And why didn't I think of this before, when Mom had a full-time job?

I look over at Artie, who doesn't ever question her life. Her artistic parents who both work from home. Her handsome, popular brother. Her beautiful, brilliant sister who is applying only to Ivy League colleges. She doesn't even seem to notice that not everybody's family gathers around the living room to sing folk songs together after dinner while Mom strums the guitar.

When I was small, I used to wish I lived with Artie's family.

But Artie doesn't even know that her family is special, just like she doesn't realize that her hair is gorgeous and her skin is perfect. If she weren't my best friend, I'd probably hate her guts.

Someone plops down into the seat beside Artie and says, "Gimme a high five."

I pause mid-chew. It's Devon, all dimples and white teeth, and he's holding up a palm for Artie. "Don't leave me hanging," he says, and it's all I can do to not spit out my pear and high-five him myself.

But Artie just smiles and slaps his hand. "Why are we high-fiving?"

"Because they put up the callback list," Devon says. "And you and I are on it."

"That's awesome!" I choke out, and a tiny piece of pear flies out of my mouth and lands on the table. *He didn't see that*, I tell myself, but I'm not sure it's true because — for the first time in possibly ever — Devon's blue eyes are directly on mine.

I sit perfectly still, trying not to shrink under his gaze.

"Devon, this is Hayley," Artie says.

"Hi." Devon smiles.

"Congratulations on the callback," I tell him. "That's great."

"Thanks," he says warmly. "It doesn't mean anything yet, but . . ."

"But it could," I put in, which makes him smile again.

He turns to Artie. "I see your friend is an optimist."

"Usually," Artie says, and I pipe in, "I'm very optimistic!" — which makes Devon laugh and me blush.

"Callbacks are scheduled for Monday," Devon says. "I'll see you?" He climbs out of the chair.

Artie nods, and I say, "I'll make sure she's there!" Devon waves at us, then turns and walks across the cafeteria.

The minute he's out of earshot, Artie groans and covers her face in her hands.

"Whatwhatwhat?" I ask her, and for a moment I'm terrified that she's going to say, "I'm in love with Devon," but what she says is, "I was kind of hoping I wouldn't make it." Artie peeps through her fingers.

"Why?" I demand. "You have such a great voice! And you're totally overdramatic."

"Hayley!" she cries, but she's laughing. "No, it's just — I was so nervous at the last audition. And this is going to be even worse!" She twists a rope of her hair, then bites it.

"Stop flossing with your own hair," I tell her. "It's going to be great! Just try to have fun and everything will work out."

"Jeez, you really *are* optimistic," Artie says, shaking her head. "I guess I never noticed."

"I'm not optimistic; I'm realistic. You're incredibly talented."

Artie holds her hair over her eyes. "Thank you."

"You're welcome."

One hazel eye peeks out at me. "Will you come with me? To the audition?"

"I don't think they'll let me in."

"No, just — you could just wait outside." Artie's hazel eyes are huge. "Please?"

"Sure," I say. "Of course."

"You will?" Artie grabs my hand across the table. "Oh, thankyouthankyou!"

"It's no big deal," I say, but I'm secretly feeling a little bad because I said yes mainly because I knew Devon would be at the audition.

And also because I'm an amazing friend.

I guess that's why — once more — I back off from telling Artie about my little . . . thing. Crush, I guess, though I'm not sure. All I know is that there's something special about Devon, and I'm happy that I'm going to get to know him more, once Artie gets the part.

I guess maybe I *am* optimistic.

Shoot the Moon Cupcakes

(makes approximately 12 cupcakes)

These have a dreamy quality that I like. The green-tea frosting is mild and sweet, and tastes like something good is about to happen.

INGREDIENTS:

adzuki bean paste (found at specialty Asian markets or online)

1-1/4 cups all-purpose flour

2 tablespoons cornstarch

3/4 teaspoon baking powder

1/2 teaspoon baking soda

1/2 teaspoon salt

2/3 cup milk

3/4 cup sugar

1/2 cup yogurt

3/4 teaspoon vanilla extract

1/2 teaspoon almond extract

1/3 cup canola oil

INSTRUCTIONS:

1. Scoop the adzuki bean paste into walnut-sized balls, place onto wax paper, and cover with plastic until ready to use, so they don't dry out.

2. Preheat the oven to 350°F. Line a muffin pan with cupcake liners.

3. In a large bowl, sift together the flour, cornstarch, baking powder, baking soda, and salt, and mix.

4. In a separate large bowl, mix the milk with the sugar, yogurt, vanilla extract, almond extract, and oil. Then beat with a whisk or handheld mixer. Add the dry ingredients a little bit at a time, stopping occasionally to scrape the sides of the bowl, and mix until no lumps remain.

5. Fill cupcake liners two-thirds of the way, then place an adzuki paste ball in the center of each cupcake, pressing down to slightly submerge it in the batter.

6. Bake for 20–22 minutes, until cupcakes are slightly golden. Transfer to a cooling rack, and let cool completely before frosting.

Green-Tea Frosting

INGREDIENTS:

- 1/2 cup margarine, softened
- 1/2 cup shortening
- 2–4 teaspoons matcha tea powder
- 1 teaspoon vanilla extract
- 3-1/2 cups confectioners' sugar
- 1–2 tablespoons milk

INSTRUCTIONS:

1. In a large bowl, with an electric mixer, cream together the margarine and shortening. Beat in the matcha tea powder and vanilla extract.

2. Slowly beat in the confectioners' sugar, in 1/2-cup intervals, adding a little bit of milk whenever the frosting becomes too thick. Continue mixing on high speed for about 3–7 minutes, until the frosting is light and fluffy.

Something Smells

"What smells?" Mrs. McTibble asks with a sour face. She's holding her Lhasa Apso, Gwendolyn, and frowning down at our glass pastry case.

"Um, I just baked some cupcakes," I admit. "They're inspired by moon cakes — they're a traditional Chinese —"

"No wonder it smells foreign." She sniffs, then adds, "I'll take one of those."

"Really?"

"It's nice to see something different in here." She flashes a look toward my grandmother, who rolls her eyes.

"Well, if we start filling this place with new things, you and I will have to go somewhere else, Alice," Gran says, and Mrs. McTibble gives her a starched smile.

For a moment, I forget myself and reach out to pet Gwendolyn, who snaps at me, as usual. "Sorry," I mutter, then reach for a sheet of wax paper to pick up the cupcake with.

"She's a *working* dog," Mrs. McTibble reminds me sternly.

Right. Usually, dogs aren't allowed in the café — it's a health-code thing. But Gwendolyn wears a blue "helper dog" jacket at all times when she's here, even though her helper status is pretty questionable. I mean, Mrs. McTibble carries her everywhere, and the old lady doesn't seem to have any problems with her sight, hearing, or sharp tongue. So what's Gwendolyn helping with, besides being Mrs. McTibble's match in the grouch department?

I place the cupcake on a white plate and take it over to Mrs. McTibble's usual table, beside the bay window. We don't usually offer table service, but Mrs. McTibble is Mrs. McTibble, so we do things her way. She takes a prim little bite of the cupcake, and her frown lines soften. "Thank you, dear," she says.

"Y-you're welcome." I stammer a little, because (a) Mrs. McTibble has never said thank you to me before and (b) she's never called me dear before. She offers a little piece of cake to Gwendolyn, who sniffs and wags before gobbling it up.

Well, that was an unexpected triumph.

I help two good-looking college guys with their order — one gets a cupcake and the other a scone — and then wipe down the glossy dark wood counter. Gran isn't paying me much to help in the café, but I don't really care. I just like to be here, with the light streaming in through the bay window and the heavy wood tables. Gran has hung the walls with faded pictures of English flowers, and the whole place seems very quaint and old, which it is. She has been running the Tea Room for over twenty years. Mom told me that it was popular for a while in the late 1990s, but now it's mostly just a fixture on the block that survives because of our regulars.

The bell over the door jingles, and my mother walks in. She's wearing her red silk shirt and black pants, and has a black jacket slung over one arm. Her shoes are polished and her hair looks perfect, but her face seems harried. She looks at my grandmother, then at me. "I blew it," she announces. Then she tosses her jacket over the smooth counter and steps to the coffeemaker.

"What happened?" I ask as Mom reaches for a teacup.

Mom shakes her head and pours coffee into the cup. "I snorted water through my nose."

"What?" I screech, just as Gran says, "Oh, Margaret — how *could* you?"

"Mother! I didn't do it on purpose," Mom says, and it's funny to hear her sound just like me. In fact, snorting water through her nose — that sounds *just* like me. I guess that sort of thing is genetic, like brown eyes and an inability to play soccer.

"It's just — they gave me a bottle of water. And the interview was really going well, I thought. Then I said, 'Believe me, Mr. Alper, if I can corral two kids and handle a full-time job, which I did for seven years, then I can organize your office.' And I took a big drink of water. But then he said, 'Sounds like you're overqualified,' and he had this dead serious look on his face, and it — I just laughed — but my mouth was full of water —"

"Oh, no," I say. Really, I'm horrified.

"It came pouring down right in my lap. Nice guy — he dashed off to get me some paper towels."

"That makes it worse," I say.

Mom sighs and takes a swig from her cup, then makes a face and spits the coffee back. "Mother! What is this?" she demands.

"It's coffee," Gran replies.

"When did you brew it?"

Gran looks at the clock. "Eight this morning."

"That's almost eight hours ago!" Mom puts the teacup on the counter. "Mother — don't you know you need to have gourmet coffee these days?"

"I'm English," Gran replies. "What do I know about coffee? Besides, this is a tea shop."

"If you want to have customers, you need coffee. Good

coffee. In mugs, not teacups." Mom looks at me as if to say, *Am I right?*

"And iced coffee, maybe," I suggest.

"This is why I need your help!" Gran insists.

Just then, I hear a laugh. When I look over, I see that the two handsome college guys have pulled their table over beside Mrs. McTibble's. She's smiling and telling them a story that involves a lot of gesturing.

"What's that all about?" Mom asks.

"Cupcakes make people happy," I tell her.

My grandmother raises a delicate eyebrow. "People, but not dogs," she says, as Mrs. McTibble's gesticulating is clearly putting Gwendolyn out of sorts.

The door jingles again, and in walks Chloe. She is looking like her usual rumpled self — I swear that her clothes are never wrinkled when she leaves in the morning, so it's always a little odd to see her come home with her shirt untucked, her socks covered in dirt, and one of her braids undone, as she is now. She holds the door for an African-American boy wearing small oval spectacles and a serious look. They don't speak to each other, but they step up to the counter at the same time.

"Can I help you?" I ask the boy.

"I'm with her." His voice is a whisper, and his hands are shoved deep into his pockets, so he juts his chin at Chloe.

"Okay, so what'll it be?" I ask Chloe.

"We'll have two of whatever's good," she says.

I catch Mom and Gran exchanging a smile and I whip out two pieces of wax paper. I place one of Gran's ginger-pear scones on one plate, and a Shoot the Moon cupcake on the other. "Who wants which?" I ask, holding out the plates.

"We'll share," Chloe announces, reaching for both.

Chloe's companion chooses a table in the corner. He dusts it off with a paper napkin as she sets down the plates.

"A new friend," Mom whispers in my ear, and I smile.

"Don't stare at them," I tell her. "Don't make a big deal out of it."

"Of course not." Mom bustles off, and I start making notes for a new cupcake. A friendship cupcake. Maybe two different flavors swirled together?

"Hayley?" Chloe is standing before me, an empty plate in her hand. "I need another cupcake, please."

"You're done already?" I ask, opening the case.

"It's for Horatio," Chloe explains.

I hesitate a moment, then give her the cupcake. "Okay."

She flashes a huge grin at me, then lopes off to join her real friend and her imaginary one at their table in the corner.

Confession:
I Hate Mean People

Oh, I'm not talking about Mrs. McTibble. She's grouchy, but I don't think she's mean. The only person she really makes unhappy is herself.

No, the people I'm talking about are the kind who could be mean to a sweet eight-year-old.

There are four elementary schools in Northampton — Branson School, Jefferson Street School, Waterville Road Elementary, and Cunningham Elementary. Chloe used to go to Cunningham. But this year, Mom switched her into Branson, even before we moved. Why?

Chloe was getting teased.

All last year, there were three girls who made Chloe's life miserable. They were only in the second grade, so I can't really call them the "popular girls." They were just nasty for no reason. One of them even punched Chloe in the stomach, but when Chloe told the teacher, the other two acted like my sister was making it up. But I know Chloe — she has an impressive imagination, but she's not a liar.

The worst part of it is that those three girls used to be Chloe's best friends. But one of them turned on her, and then the other two did, too. And it was awful. Chloe was too sad and too shy to try to make friends with anyone else. Those mean girls teased her for her clothes, her freckles — even the fact that our parents were getting divorced. Chloe started to shrivel up under their words, like a plant that isn't getting any water or light. It didn't matter what I said, or what my mom said. It didn't matter that we loved her. She tried to ignore them, but how could she? She was lonely.

So she spent more and more time with Horatio.

I guess that's why Mom and I are kind of freaking out that she's got a new friend, maybe. A real friend.

It's just been so long.

Oh, please. Please let this be a nice, normal friend.

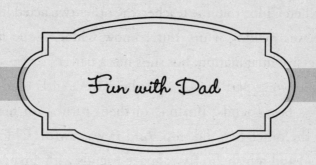

Fun with Dad

$\mathcal{M}$y dad pulls the Lexus to the curb and honks the horn, as usual. The first couple of times Dad picked us up, he came inside and we all suffered through an awkwardly polite conversation between him and Mom. But since we've moved in with Gran, he just honks the horn. I guess the thought of interacting with his ex-mother-in-law just put him over the edge.

"Here he is," I announce from my perch beside the upstairs bay window. Chloe comes dashing out of our room and through the apartment door.

"Aren't you going to give me a hug?" Mom calls after her. I hear a loud squeak as Chloe's sneakers skid to a halt, followed by thundering footsteps. Chloe zips back into the living room, gives Mom a quick squeeze, and hurries out again.

"Tell your father that I want you home by seven," Mom tells me.

"Okay." I sigh. Mom holds out her arms — one hand carefully holding a coffee mug — and I give her a hug. Then it's out the door and down the stairs after Chloe. She's giving Dad a bear hug on the sidewalk. I just wave awkwardly.

"Hello, Hayley," Dad says. We're kind of formal with each other lately.

"Hi." I reach for the car door, and my dad's face contorts, like I'm about to touch a hot stove, but I've already yanked it open. A young woman with jet-black hair and light brown eyes looks up at me, surprised. "Oh, sorry," I say, and slam the door.

Dad and I stare at each other for a long, weird moment. Then I look back at the car. "Oh," I say again. "Wait — this *is* our car."

My brain isn't working right. I'm confused. What's this person doing in our car?

"Who's that?" Chloe asks.

Dad hurries over to the door and pulls it open. The young woman is still there, smiling now. She's glamorous in a short tweed skirt and high heels, and her eyes twinkle under sparkly brown shadow.

"Girls, this is Annie Montri," Dad says. "Annie, this is Hayley."

Annie sticks out her hand, which is at an awkward angle, because she's strapped in by her seat belt. I shake her hand, and Chloe waves enthusiastically. "Hi, I'm Chloe!" she says, then climbs into the backseat like everything's normal.

I look over at Dad, but he doesn't meet my eyes. He just goes around the back of the car to the driver's seat, leaving me to climb in with Chloe. Which I do, like a good daughter.

But in my head, I'm pitching a crazy screamfit, like, "Oh, so I can't bring someone, but you can? What happened to '*This is our time together, Hayley*'? You are so full of it! Is this your *girlfriend*, Dad?"

I'm seething there in the backseat while Chloe is looking out the window, humming along with the radio. The silence in the car is dense, like a thick fog, clouding everything.

Finally, I can't take it anymore. "So, how do you two know each other?"

"Annie's a paralegal at the firm."

I guess Annie doesn't want me to get the wrong idea, because she smiles over at Dad and pats him on the knee.

I want to hurl.

She twists in her seat to give me a big smile, flashing white teeth and red lipstick. "I've never been apple picking," she says.

"You'll love it!" This is Chloe, who is beaming at Annie.

What's wrong with you? I wonder, glaring at my sister. She's so shy around kids her age — why is she being so friendly to this random person?

"I think it's so hilarious that Americans do this for fun," Annie says. "Where I'm from, we leave this sort of thing to laborers!" Then she laughs like someone who's just taken a class in how to laugh — head thrown back and hahahaha!

Wow. I didn't realize it was possible for me to like her less than I did two minutes ago, but I do.

"Where are you from?" Chloe asks.

Oh, jeez, Chloe, who cares? I want to tell her, but I just cock my head and try to act fascinated.

"My family is from Thailand. We came to America when I was twelve." She runs her long red fingernails through her glossy black hair. *Who does she think she is?* I wonder, eyeing her elegant outfit. *A supermodel?* She looks really young to me, like ten years younger than Dad. *Maybe people will think we're out with our dad and our babysitter. I hope.*

"You don't have an accent," Chloe notes.

"Thank you."

Even that irks me. My grandmother has an accent. Mr. Malik has an accent. What's wrong with an accent? Nothing!

I guess Annie has noticed that I'm not contributing to the conversation, because she turns to me and says, "So,

Hayley — do you have any crushes on boys?" She smiles, like we're best friends at a slumber party.

"No."

More uncomfortable silence. After a minute, Annie asks Chloe what her favorite subject is, and for a while they chat happily about science. Dad volunteers, "Hayley's favorite subject is English."

Not true, but I don't argue.

"What's your favorite book?" Annie asks.

"I like a lot of books." The end. And . . . silence. Yay. It's like we're starting a silence collection.

Finally, Dad pulls into the dirt driveway at Stone's Throw Farm, and we get out of the car.

"Oh, how charming," Annie says as she looks at the farm stand.

My dad walks over to her, and she slips her hand into his.

I grab two half-peck baskets and hand one to Chloe. The guy at the farm stand — apple-cheeked and Mohawked — smiles at me and says that the Empires are ready, so I head down the hill. Chloe runs ahead and dances down a path between McIntosh trees.

"Why don't you guys just wait up here?" I snap. I know my voice is harsh, but I don't want them with us. I never should have said yes to apple picking.

Annie looks hurt, and my dad's face gets stern. "Go ahead, Hayley," he says. "We're right behind you." Dad takes a basket, too, and he and Annie slowly start to totter down the hill after us. I guess the four-inch heels aren't seeming like such a great idea to her now.

It rained last night, and my sneakers squelch over the muddy grass as I follow Chloe to the Empires. These are my favorite apples — they're an heirloom variety, very small and sweet. Not many people grow them.

I hear someone cry out behind me, and I turn to see Annie clutching at Dad, one of her heels buried completely in the mud. Annie tries to pull her foot up, but her toes pop out of the shoe, and the heel stays stuck in the ground. She takes another step forward and the other heel sinks into the mud.

I feel myself smile a smug little smile. I'm horrible, but I can't help it. Dad reaches down to pull out the shoe, and the heel breaks off.

My dad scowls at me. "Hayley! Get over here and help!" Like it's *my* fault!

I have no idea what he thinks I can do, but I obey. Chloe comes dashing out of the trees and takes in the situation. She looks at Annie's red face and her glistening eyes, and says, "Oh, Annie, your beautiful shoes!" She runs over to give Annie a hug.

Annie stands there in stocking feet, my sister's arms wrapped around her, and pats Chloe's head awkwardly. "They're just shoes," Annie says, even though she looks humiliated and sad.

"But they were so *pretty*," Chloe says. "And you got all dressed up to meet us!"

The words are like a knife to my heart. An image flashes in my mind: Annie, trying to choose an outfit she'll wear to meet her boyfriend's daughters, having no idea what apple picking is like.

"The apples here are the best in the world." Chloe reaches into her basket and gives one to Annie, who takes a bite. Annie smiles and nods while she crunches the sweet fruit.

"Delicious," Annie says. Her face is still flushed, but her tears seem to be drying up.

I lean over and carefully twist the broken heel from the ground. I hand it to my father, who says, "Thanks."

"Well, you can't go around in your tights," I say to Annie.

"Why don't you girls go pick apples," Dad suggests. "We'll meet you at the stand. Annie and I can get some doughnuts."

"Ooh — cider doughnuts!" Chloe cries. "I'm going to pick super fast!" She gives Annie another squeeze, then dashes off again.

I watch as Dad pats Annie on the back. He is carrying her muddy, ruined shoes in one hand as they turn and start back up the hill.

I guess I got what I wanted. I can pick apples with my sister in peace.

So why do I feel so horrible?

Apple Cupcakes

(makes approximately 12–15 cupcakes)

This is the ideal cupcake to make on a rainy fall day. Extra points for a cup of apple cider, too.

INGREDIENTS:
- 1 tablespoon margarine
- 3 tablespoons brown sugar
- 2 large apples, any variety, peeled and chopped (about 1/2-inch to 1-inch pieces)
- 1/2 teaspoon ground cinnamon
- 1 cup milk
- 1 teaspoon apple cider vinegar
- 1-1/4 cups all-purpose flour
- 3/4 teaspoon baking powder
- 1/2 teaspoon baking soda
- 1/2 teaspoon salt
- 3/4 cup sugar
- 1 teaspoon vanilla extract
- 1/3 cup canola oil

INSTRUCTIONS:

1. Preheat the oven to 350°F. Line a muffin pan with foil cupcake liners. (Paper ones are too sticky! If you don't have foil ones, grease the inside of the muffin pan instead.)

2. In a skillet, on low heat, melt the margarine and brown sugar together. Then add the apple chunks and ground cinnamon, and sauté until nice and soft. Remove from heat and let cool.

3. Whisk the milk and vinegar together in a bowl and set aside for a few minutes to curdle.

4. In a large bowl, sift together the flour, baking powder, baking soda, and salt, and mix.

5. In a separate large bowl, mix together the curdled milk, sugar, vanilla extract, and oil. Then beat with a whisk or handheld mixer. Add the dry ingredients a little bit at a time, and mix until no lumps remain.

6. Spoon apple chunks into each cupcake liner, enough to cover the bottom.

7. Fill cupcake liners two-thirds of the way and bake for 20–22 minutes. Transfer to a cooling rack, and let cool completely before frosting.

Vanilla Frosting

INGREDIENTS:

- 1/2 cup margarine, softened
- 1/2 cup shortening
- 1 teaspoon vanilla extract
- 3-1/2 cups confectioners' sugar
- 1–2 tablespoons milk

INSTRUCTIONS:

1. In a large bowl, with an electric mixer, cream together the margarine and shortening. Beat in the vanilla extract.
2. Slowly beat in the confectioners' sugar, in 1/2-cup intervals, adding a little bit of milk whenever the frosting becomes too thick. Continue mixing on high speed for about 3–7 minutes, until the frosting is light and fluffy.

Poor Mom

"Are you making apple cupcakes?" Mom asks as she walks into Gran's tiny kitchen. Because this is just a small batch, I'm baking them upstairs in the apartment instead of down with the huge industrial mixer. Mom spots the two half-peck baskets on the counter, one of which is half-empty. Her face falters for a minute, and then she recovers. "Oh. Did you go apple picking with Dad?"

"Kind of."

"Kind of?"

"Chloe and I did most of the picking."

Notice that I do not mention Annie. That's because she is irrelevant to the conversation I'm having with my mother, in case you're wondering.

Stooping over, I pull open the oven and reach for a mitt. The cupcakes are perfect domes rising over the rims of the red foil wrappers, and the air is thick with the scent of cinnamon.

"They look gorgeous," Mom says.

"It's your recipe."

"Which I got off a bag of flour about twenty years ago."

"Really?" That makes me giggle — and also makes sense. Mom doesn't bake much — she's always left that to Gran.

"Are Marco and Artie coming over?" Mom asks.

"It's Game Night."

"I guess it is."

Marco, Artie, and I have been getting together every other Saturday for two years. It started out because our parents liked to get together for dinner parties pretty often, and we kids would get bored. So we'd all go down to the basement to play games. Artie likes these annoying games like Scrabble or Boggle or Bananagrams — anything with words. Marco and I prefer games where armies invade countries — Axis & Allies, Risk, that kind of thing. Tonight is a Bananagrams night, but that's okay because sometimes Marco tries to cheat by making up words, which always makes me laugh.

Mom gets the confectioners' sugar from the top shelf — she knows I'll need it for the frosting. "I'm glad you guys are still having Game Night."

"Why wouldn't we?"

"No reason, I guess."

I lift each cupcake carefully onto a cooling rack. Of course, I know what she means. Game Night has always been held in our basement, which is huge and has an awesome, thick carpet that's great for lying on, especially if you're half-propped on an enormous pillow.

But we don't live in that house anymore. Mom doesn't have dinner parties with Marco's and Artie's parents anymore, either. That stopped a few months ago, once the divorce was announced.

But yesterday I asked Marco and Artie if they were coming over for Game Night, and both said yes, so here we are. I dump the margarine and shortening into the bowl, and turn on the electric mixer.

"Ooh, can I have one?" Chloe asks as she rushes in. She reaches for a cupcake, and I give her hand a playful swat.

"They aren't even frosted yet."

"Did you have fun apple picking, sweetie?" Mom asks.

"Yes! But I don't think Annie did."

I turn on the mixer, but it doesn't stop Mom from asking, "Who's Annie?"

"Dad's friend," Chloe says nonchalantly. Then she asks, "Can I lick the beater when you're done?"

"No," I snap.

"Why not?"

Because you've broken Mom's heart! I sneak a glance at Mom, who looks shell-shocked. But she notices me watching, and forces a smile. She doesn't say *You didn't mention Annie.* Now I wish I had. Not mentioning Annie has made her seem important, when she's really just irrelevant.

Irrelevant!

"*Please* can I lick one?" Chloe begs, and I snap off the beaters without a word and hand one over.

Mom and I look at each other for a moment. "I see," she says finally, then touches my shoulder very, very gently, almost like she's whispering a secret, before she walks out of the room.

Confession:
That. Was. Awkward.

$\mathcal{L}$et me tell you a little about my dad.

Two years ago, he decided that he didn't want to be an assistant district attorney anymore. So he got a job at a fancy law firm, which is where he works now.

It's in Springfield, which is about a thirty-minute commute. Not long. But a lot longer than the old, five-minute one.

Anyway, so Dad started working at this nice law firm. I remember the first time I went there — the elevators are chrome and shiny and so fast you feel like you're zooming to the top floor. Everyone was beautifully dressed: The men's shoes were shined and the women had manicures. Let me just explain something about Northampton, where I live. It's pretty casual. Casual, as in, if your orange Crocs match your orange fleece, you're stylish. So this place seemed really fancy and elegant, and they had this pale-gray carpet that I figured they probably had to vacuum every five seconds.

Well, what happened when Dad started working there was that his clothes got nice real fast. He bought these shirts that had to go out to the dry cleaner's, instead of just getting washed at home, and he started a cuff-link collection. Then he got new shoes. Then he got a fancy new phone that he was always typing on and staring at, even at dinner or when the rest of us were watching TV.

The car was the next to go. Out went the ten-year-old Toyota. In came the sporty silver Lexus.

"I need it," Dad would say. "The firm expects you to project a certain image. I can't go visit clients in an old Toyota; they'll think I don't know what I'm doing."

Next up, new vacation. For years, we had always rented the same little lake cottage up in Goshen. Right by the "Goshen Ocean," which is a peaceful lake just twenty minutes from our house. But last summer, we went to Spain.

Dad kept talking about how great it was, but what I remember is that it was hot.

Anyway, when we came back in the fall, Dad decided that we should remodel our kitchen. "These floors are from 1953," he said. And it was true, although I'd never heard him complain about the floors before. So he hired a contractor, and for three weeks, we couldn't even eat in our kitchen because we had no cabinets, no stove, no fridge. Not even plates or cups — everything had been boxed up.

Mom was worried about the cost, but Dad didn't listen to her.

"I'm making all this money," Dad kept saying. "Let's enjoy it!"

The only problem was that he never really seemed to be enjoying it. About a week after the kitchen was finished, Mom made chicken parm, Chloe's favorite. Chloe was helping Mom with the salad, and we were about to have dinner — our first in the new kitchen. Dad and I were setting the table, and when he pulled open the silverware drawer, it came clean out — the forks and knives and spoons clattered all over the new Mexican-tile floor. Dad cursed and kicked the drawer and yanked out his cell phone so he could shout at the contractor. Chloe started crying and Mom put her arms around her, and I just stood there, looking at our gleaming kitchen — the new stainless steel fridge, the new stove, the new wooden cabinets — the kitchen that we were supposed to enjoy.

Two weeks later, Dad and Mom were going out on a date. When Mom came out, dressed in dark jeans and a white shirt, I heard Dad ask, "Is that what you're wearing?" She said yes and that was the end of it, but I remember wondering if Mom was going to be the next thing to get "improved."

But it didn't quite work out that way. Instead, Dad moved out in the spring. And now he's seeing Annie. I wonder if she's supposed to be the new, improved version of Mom.

I wonder if that's what Mom is thinking, too.

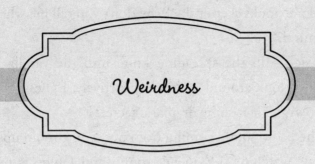

Weirdness

"And so then a giant spider landed on my head and tried to eat my brain."

"What?" I snap to attention and cock my head at Marco, who is helping me frost apple cupcakes. "Spider — what?"

He gives me a sly smile. "Oh, so you *are* listening."

I feel myself blush, the red flame creeping across my cheeks. "Sorry."

"I've been talking for the past ten minutes, and you haven't said anything except 'mmm,' 'hmm,' or 'mmm-hmm.'"

"I heard what you were saying," I protest, but the moment the words are out of my mouth, I realize that I have zero idea what Marco has been talking about. Soccer? English class? My blush flares brighter when I realize it could be anything. "Okay, tell me again."

Marco looks skeptical. "Why don't you tell me what's on *your* mind?"

I sigh, dip the spreading knife into the vanilla frosting, then look around — kind of furtively, I guess, because Marco says, "Is it some dramatic secret?"

There's no sound coming from my mom's room upstairs, Gran is watching TV in her room, and Chloe is over at her friend's house. We've learned his name, by the way. It's Rupert, and he lives three doors down from us. Anyway, I keep my voice low and say, "Kind of."

Marco's eyebrows fly up, and he looks like he isn't sure he really wants to hear what I have to say. I blurt out, "My dad introduced me to . . . I think . . . his girlfriend."

Marco winces. "Oh, weird."

"I know."

"Are you sure she's not a friend?"

"She put her hand on his knee."

Marco looks horrified, and then pretends to barf into the frosting bowl.

"That's how I felt," I tell him.

"I'm sorry, but even watching my parents *hug* kind of gives me the creeps," he admits. "I really can't imagine them putting their hands on random people's knees."

I giggle, partly because I'm relieved that someone under-stands, and also partly because I start imagining Marco's par-ents putting their hands on random people's knees — like in a bus or at the library.

"What's she like?"

"Pretty," I say. "Kind of young."

"Even grosser," Marco says.

"I know."

"Is she nice?"

I'm about to say no, but I stop to think it over for a moment. She did try to talk to us. And she smiled a lot. And Chloe likes her. "Maybe," I admit. "Does that mean I have to like her?"

"No." Marco places his neatly frosted cupcake on the counter and picks up another. "I was just curious." He looks at the wall clock.

"She's late."

"More than usual," Marco says.

"Well, she isn't just walking through the backyard."

As if she senses us talking about her, the phone rings. "It's Artie," I tell him. "Artie, we were just talking about you."

"I'm so sorry!" Artie blurts. "I can't make it."

"What? Why not?"

"What's up?" Marco asks. He reads the disappointment on my face, and his dark eyebrows draw together in a frown.

I shake my head at him as Artie babbles, "I asked Roan on Wednesday if he could give me a ride to your house, and he said yes, but now Dad says that he's gone out and isn't coming back until ten."

"Roan flaked," I say to Marco, who rolls his eyes. Roan is Artie's seventeen-year-old brother, and kind of a space case. If he weren't a straight-A mega-nerd, I might suspect him of being on drugs.

"Why didn't she just ask my parents for a ride?" Marco sounds annoyed, and Artie hears his voice.

"Tell Marco that if I had known Roan was going to flake, I would have asked him for a ride!"

"It's okay," I say, even though it isn't.

"Look, Hayley, I'm so sorry, and I'll make it up to you, I swear."

"I hope she's apologizing," Marco says.

I nod at him and tell Artie, "Don't worry about it." I'm about to add, "There's always next time," but something holds me back. Instead, I say, "See you Monday."

"Have fun without me!" Artie chirps, and I hang up.

Marco and I look at each other for a long moment that

slowly, slowly rotates into awkwardness. "So — I guess we don't have to play Bananagrams," he says.

I let out a tense laugh. *Stop that*, I command myself, and clamp my lips shut. "So." I take out two plates and place a cupcake on each one. "Should we play Risk?"

"No fun with two people."

"Battleship?"

Marco laughs, and says, "Yeah," but he sounds sarcastic, and neither one of us makes a move toward the living room.

"Maybe we should just watch a movie or something," I suggest.

"Sure."

So we take our cupcakes and head into the living room. Marco looks around. "This is nice," he says, and I remember with a sudden flash that he's never been here before.

Of course. He's been to the café downstairs — but never upstairs, to my grandmother's apartment. Her living room *is* nice — full of elegant furniture that she inherited from her own mother, and beautifully kept. Gran is one of those old-school housekeepers who, like, mop every day.

"Yeah, it's pretty." I look on the shelf. Our DVDs are only partially unpacked, so I have a pretty lame selection to offer. We finally decide on an old musical, and I put it in, then sit down on the couch beside Marco.

The music begins, and I take a bite out of my cupcake, trying not to think about how weird this is. Over the past two years, Game Night has been canceled before . . . but it has never, ever been just me and Marco.

Still, we're good friends.

So why should this be weird?

Yet it *is* weird. Here we are — in a house that's not my house, watching a movie on Game Night, without Artie. It's all wrong, like a puzzle put together by a toddler, upside down and backward.

The movie blares on, but I can hardly watch it. I wish I could just go to bed.

I eat my cupcake. What else is there for me to do?

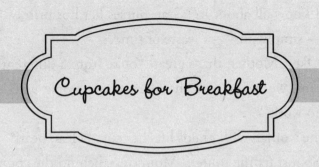

Cupcakes for Breakfast

"Is anyone else having trouble with the Wi-Fi?" Mom looks up from her computer and peers around the café.

A woman with braided hair sips her coffee and gives Mom a wry smile. "The Wi-Fi never works here."

"What?" Mom looks over at Gran, who gives her a sheepish smile. "Mother, you can't post a sign that says you have Wi-Fi and then not have wireless. People need to use their computers."

"What for?" Gran demands. "So they can poke each other?"

"Gran!" I clap a hand over my mouth, but my laugh escapes anyway.

"That's right, I know about poking," Gran says to me. "I know all about Friendbook!"

"Facebook," I say.

"I know all about it." Gran purses her lips primly. "And it is — simply put — a waste of time."

"Okay, Mother, that's great. You're from a different millennium, we get it. But there are some people who come here to work."

The woman with braids lifts her cup. "Hear, hear!"

"So just fix the router." Mom steps behind the counter.

"I can't figure the darn thing out," Gran admits. She turns to me. "Excuse me."

Yes, that's right — my grandmother says "Excuse me" whenever she says "darn." I smile to show that I'm not horribly offended.

Mom opens the cupboard where the wireless is hidden. "Well, it might help to plug it in." Mom's voice is dry. "And it also might help to blow some of the dust off this thing." A red light flashes, then two green lights. Mom shuts the cupboard doors and goes back to her computer. She taps at the keyboard. "Working," she announces.

A guy in a faded concert T-shirt and jeans walks in and flashes a smile at Gran. He's got that raggedy student look that's so popular around here. There are five colleges within twenty minutes of Northampton: Smith is right here in town; Amherst, Hampshire, and the main campus of the University of Massachusetts are in Amherst; Mount Holyoke is in South Hadley. Sometimes it seems like everybody's a student, a teacher, or a graduate.

"Do you have Wi-Fi?" the guy asks.

"Yes!" Gran says brightly, and Mom gives her a look.

"Awesome." He sniffs, his eyebrows going up. "Smells like bacon."

"That's me," I admit. "I just made these cupcakes. . . ."

"Bacon cupcakes? Are they gross?"

"I hope not. They're actually Country Morning cupcakes, with bacon and egg."

"A bacon cupcake for breakfast — that's either going to be disgusting or delicious. Gimme one of those. And a cup of coffee," he adds. He slings his backpack off his shoulder and puts it down on a table, then pulls out some money to pay.

I add a tiny piece of bacon to the top of the cupcake and set it on a plate. It's still warm from the oven. I can't help biting my lip as he tastes it. I mean, I think they're good — but the bacon was my idea, and I might be insane.

"Whoa." The guy gives me a huge grin. "These are crazy! Can you put four more in a box for me?"

"Lunch?" I ask.

"Housemates," he says, and I have to admit that I'm relieved.

He sits down to work for a while, staring at his screen

and munching his cupcake nonstop. The coffeepot is almost empty, so I rinse it out and brew a fresh one. Then I decorate the chalkboard out front: CUPCAKE OF THE DAY: COUNTRY BREAKFAST! A DELICIOUS BLEND OF BACON, EGG, AND PANCAKE WITH MAPLE-SYRUP FROSTING. COFFEE OF THE DAY: PERUVIAN BLEND. COME CHECK OUT OUR WI-FI! Then I draw autumn leaves around the edges. The sky is a deep blue, and the day is warm. It's one of those perfect October days that feels like one of September's leftovers. When the weather gets cold, maybe I'll make pumpkin cupcakes. I seriously love pumpkin.

I let the sun soak into my skin, warming me. It's almost ten in the morning, and the town is already humming. People are walking about, peering in windows, strolling and smiling. A middle-aged couple holding hands stops to read my sign. I hold the door for them as they detour into our café.

When I step back inside, Mom is behind the counter helping herself to another cup of coffee. "We're going to need to get a real coffeemaker — an industrial one," Mom says. "Something easier to manage." I can see the wheels turning behind her eyes, and she moves toward her computer — to do research on coffeemakers, no doubt, while Gran helps the customers, charming them with her British accent.

It was a weird Saturday, but now it's Sunday, and all's right with the world.

Confession:
My Mother Is an ~~Awesome~~ Office Manager

Here are some facts about my mother:

Her closet is organized by season, type of clothing, and color.

She keeps our grocery list on her computer. Items we regularly buy are listed in order of where they appear in the store. Then she just checks off whether we need it or not.

She has only two colors of socks: white (for exercising) and black (for all other situations). All the same brand. She replaces them once a year.

She never forgets a birthday, but just in case, she has all of her friends and relatives listed in her computer, with a pop-up reminder seven days beforehand so she can go out and get a card.

Are you getting the picture? She's the most practical,

organized person I know. Chloe and I like to joke that she's like one of the X-Men. Organizatrix, or something.

She's already using her powers on the café. Any office she works for will run so smoothly, they'll think they've been greased.

I just want her to get a job soon.

Last week, I overheard her on the phone with her sister, my aunt, Denise. "I just never thought I'd be forty-seven, divorced, and living with Mother again," she said, and her voice sounded so heavy, like a stone falling through the deep ocean. "I don't even have a job. I feel like a —" She didn't finish, and I heard Aunt Denise's voice soothing her through the phone lines.

Yes, a job would be good.

Soon.

Feeling Drifty

It's weird to walk into Adams Middle School by myself.

Artie and Marco and I all took the same bus last year, and we still take the same bus this year — only I get on earlier. But this morning, neither of my friends were waiting when the driver stopped up the street from Artie's house. A sixth grader named Eve got on, and then we sailed away.

It's raining, so Artie probably got a ride. Maybe they took Marco, too.

But that left me alone, and I felt a little drifty — like a balloon that's been let go and sails off to float on the wind.

The hallways are crowded and bustling as I make my way down the wide corridor. As I near the seventh-grade lockers, I see Meghan Markerson walking out of Dean Whittier's office. They're both laughing. She catches my eye and gives me a little finger-wave, but the dean of academics doesn't glance my way. It's funny to see them together — Dean Whittier, tall and lanky, with a trim beard and a sweater vest, and Meghan, dressed in a red plaid skirt and black hoodie.

What could they possibly be laughing about?

It's a mystery to ponder as I toss my books in my locker and grab my notebook for first period.

Artie smiles and waves as I walk into homeroom, but she's already sitting with Kelley Kane and Chang Xiao. I know them vaguely, in that way that you kind of know everyone in your grade, but I don't think I've ever had a conversation with either one of them. Chang and Kelley are dramaramas, and they look like it: Chang always wears this amazing dark eye shadow and eyeliner that I'd never be able to pull off, and Kelley has a thing for stylish jeans. Everyone says Chang is really funny, so I feel a little outclassed when I walk over to join them.

"Hey, do you guys know Hayley?" Artie asks as I slip into the seat behind hers.

"Sure," Chang says.

"She was in our French class last year," Kelley adds.

I wonder who they're thinking of. I've never taken French, but decide to let it pass.

"I heard they're going to do a second round of callbacks," Kelley says to Artie.

"Oh, ugh, that is *so* Ms. Lang," Chang gripes. "She's such a drama queen." She says it so dramatically that I feel confident she's qualified to know.

"I don't think I can handle another audition." Artie glances at me. "I get nervous before each one."

"That's just a rumor; I wouldn't listen to it." Chang gives Kelley a dry, heavy-lidded look. "Personally, I never listen to anything Kelley says."

"Chang!" Kelley tosses an eraser playfully at her friend, and I'm having the same feeling I had before with Devon — that feeling that I am watching a conversation happening inside the house next door. So close, but so . . . not part of it.

I see Meghan slip in right before the first bell, and a moment later, the PA crackles and morning announcements begin. Blah, blah, something about a pep rally; anyone wanting to join the chorus; don't forget teacher in-service day. And then, "The administration also wishes to inform the students that this Friday there will be a special election. It has come to the attention of the principal and vice principal that a number of students are unhappy with the mascot. And so, this Friday during homeroom, we will hold a vote on whether to retain the Purple Pintos or adopt a new mascot of your choice."

The class goes wild, with people stomping and clapping.

Meghan stands up and takes a bow, blowing kisses all over the place. She has a goofy grin on her face.

Artie looks at me. She's clapping, but grimacing my way. "I am not voting for the Giant Squids," she says.

"How about the Crustaceans?" Chang suggests, and Kelley pipes up, "The Oysters!"

"How about the Purple Porpoises?" This is Chang again. Kelley and Artie crack up. I laugh, too. Somehow, the idea of going from the Purple Pintos to the Purple Porpoises strikes me as funny.

"I really can't believe we're going to take up school time with this election," Artie says. I get what she's saying.

School mascots aren't really important. Except that they represent us. So, in that way, I guess they are.

Picking a mascot is actually kind of hard, once you think about it.

What are we? Proud, like eagles? Fighters, like wolverines?

Personally, I think I'm more like a lesser galago. That's this wide-eyed, long-tailed African lemur-type thing I saw at the zoo once. They're furry and a little silly-looking, not too threatening. But I don't claim to represent the whole school.

"Maybe we could be the Sloths," I suggest, and that makes Artie and her new friends crack up.

"I couldn't care less what they pick," Chang says, as if she isn't one of us.

"Anything but the Giant Squids," Artie agrees. "Or the Purple Pintos."

I nod.

But I don't really mean it.

Confession:
I Think the Giant Squids Would Be an Awesome Mascot!

Seriously — can't you just see the football helmets?

More Weirdness

It's always a little eerie to be in the school building after classes are over. I can hear the echoes of my footsteps as I click down the hall. A clump of three sixthies hangs by the lockers, laughing about who knows what. Students have covered the glass trophy cases with taped-up posters. SCREAMING MACHOS! reads one. GO, ELECTROLYTES! reads another. FIGHTING EAGLES has come undone, and is half-lying on the floor. Above it is a plain white poster with a large, cartoonish gray squid cut from construction paper. No words, but everyone knows what it means.

It's Friday, and the elections for school mascot were held during lunch. There was a small contingent to keep the Purple Pintos, but most of the school seemed excited by the idea of having a new mascot. I voted for the Squids, of course.

Now I'm making my way down the hall, past classroom 108, aka Auditionville. I catch up to Artie just before she goes in.

"Good luck," I say to her.

"Break a leg," she corrects me.

I can't make myself say that, so I just smile. "You'll do great."

She flashes me a sour face, then gives me a quick hug before turning to join the other auditionees. A group of five guys — including Devon — is singing a cappella in the corner. Others are poring over scripts, or just sitting and chatting. Everyone looks happy . . . and artsy. Artie's wearing a jean miniskirt and a brown top that brings out the deep tones of her auburn hair. She's also rocking a new pair of silver flats that I've never seen. She looks cool.

She looks like one of them.

I decide to go watch Marco practice for a little while. I have a surprise for him, anyway.

The afternoon light is dim as I swing open one of the double doors. It's a cloudy day, strangely damp, and the cool air clings to me. It's colder than I expected, and I dig one hand into a pocket of my Windbreaker. The other is wrapped around the handles of a paper shopping bag. I catch a whiff of woodsmoke in the air; someone is burning firewood. It is the first time I've smelled it this fall.

I cross the wide sidewalks and cut through the grass to the practice fields. Marco's dark hair streaks toward the far goal. He's running a drill, along with the rest of the team. There's a clump of dirt on the back of his calf, and it flashes against his olive skin as his legs pump. One leg goes out, makes contact with the black-and-white ball — it sails just over the goalie's gloved hands and into the net.

I let out a whoop, and half the team turns to look in my direction, making me feel like a Grade-A weirdo. But Marco trots toward me, a smile on his face. "What's up?" he asks, slightly out of breath.

"Just waiting for Artie to finish up her audition."

"Staying for practice? It's going to be pretty boring."

"I brought a book. And I have something for you." I pull a small, round plastic container from my little shopping bag.

"Just what I needed!" Marco takes the cupcake like it's a treasure. "Don't tell the other guys — I'll get mugged. What flavor?"

"Odd Romance," I tell him. "Chocolate and ginger."

Marco and I just stand there a moment, smiling at each other from across the bench. A crack opens up in the clouds, brilliant yellow behind the gray, and a curtain of light falls onto the practice fields. I feel the breeze lift my hair slightly, and I tuck it back into place. A moment later, the cloud passes over the sun again, casting everything back into pale shadow.

Ezra hustles over and punches Marco in the arm. "Hey, are you practicing, or what?"

Marco's face blushes deep red, and he looks from Ezra to me with an odd look on his face. I feel a tickle of fear, wondering what the look means.

Ezra has been running, and his face is so pink that his freckles have disappeared. His hair is white as straw, and he looks almost like a flaming torch sending up a plume of smoke.

"I'm coming," Marco says, and bends over to shove the cupcake into his practice bag.

"What's that? Oh, a cupcake?" He smirks. "Sweets from the girlfriend, eh?"

Girlfriend? For a moment, I wonder what Ezra is talking about — and then I realize that he means me. I bust out with a honk of a laugh, which doubles back on itself into a snort. I cover my mouth and laugh even harder, out of embarrassment. "I'm not his girlfriend!" My voice is shrieky. "That's insane!"

Marco just looks at me, and I'm aware that I'm probably

humiliating him at this moment by snorting and giggling like an idiot. He probably wants to deny even knowing me at this point.

I keep expecting him to join in my giggles, but he doesn't, and my laughter slowly dies away. Marco's lips are pressed together, like they've been sewn shut, and his dark eyes are serious.

A wave of guilt breaks over me and I feel as if I've done something awful but don't know what. I'm about to ask, but Marco shoves past Ezra and walks away, right off the practice field, toward the lockers.

Ezra smiles at me, a mean little smile. "Poor little Marco," he says. Then he jogs off to join the drill.

I feel sick, because I know I've broken something that might never get repaired, and all it took was a laugh.

Confession:
Marco Kissed Me Once

It didn't seem that weird at the time. Only later. And still, sometimes I think, *Maybe that never happened and I just dreamed it.*

It was the day my parents announced that Dad was moving out. Mom and Dad called us into the family room, where our family meetings were always held. They sat me and Chloe down on the couch, and my mom proceeded to explain that while both of our parents loved us very much, they weren't going to be able to live together anymore. "Dad is moving out next week," Mom explained. "You girls will still live here, with me. And you'll see Dad on the weekends."

"You mean you're getting divorced?" Chloe asked. Her voice broke on the last word, making her sound small and helpless.

Mom's eyes welled up, and I guess she couldn't speak

because Dad chimed in and said, "Yes, Chloe. We're getting divorced."

Chloe started sobbing then, wailing and crying, and Mom hurried over to comfort her. I guess I'm a bad sister, because I remember just feeling annoyed about it. I guess I wasn't as surprised as Chloe was. I hadn't told her, but I'd caught Dad pulling sheets off the couch the week before. He'd folded them up and put them away in the closet. He didn't want us to know he'd been sleeping there, I guess.

So Chloe went on making a big, sloppy scene, and Mom finally just picked Chloe up and carried her to her room, and Dad and I were left there together.

"Do you want to talk?" Dad asked.

"What about?" Seriously, I had no idea. Like, did he want to hear about what I was studying in school?

"About . . . your feelings."

"My feelings." I wasn't feeling anything. I felt the way I felt during math. a + b = c. Mom + Chloe + Me - Dad = Our Family. That's the result. Okay. Next problem.

Dad came and sat down next to me. "It's important for you to understand that this isn't your fault."

"Why would it be my fault?" I snapped. Fury surged through me suddenly. *My fault?* Even though he'd just said that it *wasn't* my fault, I felt like he was suggesting that it really *was* my fault. I didn't want to talk about this anymore. "I have to go to the bathroom." I got up and left him there.

Of course, I didn't really have to go to the bathroom.

I just closed the lid to the toilet seat and sat down. Then I picked up a magazine. *The New Yorker*. Usually, I just skim through the cartoons, but this time I started reading a long article about a small fishing village. I finished it, then read a short story about two kids in Iowa that I liked even though I didn't really get it. Then I read a few poems.

Dad knocked on the door. "Hayley? Are you okay?"

"Fine," I said.

He paused. "Well, maybe we can talk later."

"Fine."

There was no sound for a moment. Then I heard his footsteps, walking away. I read another article, then flushed the toilet and opened the door. I guessed that Mom was still trying to get Chloe to stop crying, so I stepped outside onto our back deck.

It was a warm day in early spring — all the snow had melted except a small patch in the shadow between my house and Marco's. Three brave purple crocuses and a bunch of snowdrops were the only things blooming in our brown garden bed. Marco was in his backyard, kicking around a ball. Our yards weren't separated by a fence or anything, so when he saw me, he just said, "Hey, Hayley," and walked on over, kicking the ball the whole way.

I was perched on the top step, and he sat down beside me. "Are you okay?" he asked, looking into my face.

"My parents are getting divorced," I told him.

"Oh." He looked down at the ball in his hands, then put it on the step.

"Dad's moving out next week; Chloe's still inside, freaking out."

"I'm sorry."

"Whatever." I shrugged, but I felt my throat choking. A tear rolled from the corner of my eye, trailing down the side of my nose, and I remember thinking, *Why am I crying? I don't even feel sad.*

Marco wiped the tear away with his thumb. He placed his palms on either side of my face and tipped my forehead forward to meet his. "It's going to be okay," he whispered, and I smelled his peppermint toothpaste.

I looked into his dark eyes. "How?"

He didn't answer, but we stayed like that for a long moment, with our foreheads touching. And then his head tilted and he kissed me, a sweet, soft kiss that lingered on my lips like warm cocoa.

I felt my throat choke back a sob, and even though my

eyes were closed, I could feel hot tears leaking out of them and suddenly I was crying, not as loudly as Chloe had been, but just as violently, as if the veins in my face might burst.

"I'm sorry, I'm so sorry," Marco said, and I wanted to tell him that it was okay, but I couldn't get the words out. Then I heard a rumble and when I looked up, I saw my mom bustling out of the sliding door and heading over to me.

Marco stood up quickly. "I've got to go."

"Oh, Marco, you don't have to —" Mom said.

"It's okay." And he darted off so quickly that he left his ball behind.

Mom watched him for a moment, then looked down at me. "I didn't mean to interrupt."

I didn't answer, just wiped the tears from my face and into my hair.

"Oh, Hayley." She sat down beside me and wrapped her arms around me. "I'm so sorry that Daddy and I won't be together anymore."

The tears started again, and I said, "That's not why I'm crying."

But I didn't know why I *was* crying.

All I knew was that I couldn't stop. I put my head on Mom's soft shoulder and let her hold me for a long time. I cried, letting my nose run, letting drool spill from my mouth.

Mom didn't complain or say anything; she just hugged me and let me cry. I noticed that her sleeve was already damp, and supposed that my tears were mixing with my sister's on the fabric of my mother's shirt.

I took a few shaky breaths, and eventually managed to stop the endless flow of water. Mom took my hand and squeezed it gently, and after a while, Chloe came outside and asked what was for dinner.

I looked up and realized that the sunlight was fading.

"I don't know," Mom said.

"Can we have French toast?" Chloe's green eyes were clear, and she was smiling. I guess her despair just passed through her like a summer storm, leaving her fresher, cleaner.

Mine had rolled over me like a freight train. I was wrecked.

"Sure, Chloe," Mom said. "French toast."

So we went inside and helped her make it. It seemed dead quiet in the house until Chloe put on some awful teenybopper music that I actually found myself humming along to. I don't know where Dad was, but it was just the three of us, and I was glad.

That night, I watched the light in Marco's room until he turned it out. Then I rolled over and went to sleep and didn't dream of anything at all.

French-Toast Cupcakes

(makes approximately 12 cupcakes)

For those times you really want breakfast for dessert.

INGREDIENTS:
- 1/2 cup raisins
- 1/3 cup dark brown sugar
- 1 teaspoon cinnamon
- 2–3 tablespoons maple syrup, plus more
- 1/2 cup margarine
- 1/2 cup sugar
- 2/3 cup milk
- 1/2 cup yogurt
- 1-1/2 teaspoons vanilla extract
- 1-1/4 cups flour
- 1 teaspoon baking powder
- 1/2 teaspoon baking soda
- 1/2 teaspoon salt

INSTRUCTIONS:

1. Preheat the oven to 350°F. Line a cupcake pan with cupcake liners.
2. In a small bowl, mix together the raisins, dark

brown sugar, cinnamon, and maple syrup, and set aside.

3. In a large mixing bowl, cream the margarine and sugar with an electric mixer until light and fluffy. Add the milk, yogurt, and vanilla extract, and mix until smooth.

4. In a separate large bowl, sift together the flour, baking powder, baking soda, and salt, and mix. Slowly add the dry ingredients to the wet, and mix until smooth.

5. Fill the cupcake liners one-half to two-thirds of the way full. Then drop a spoonful of the raisin mixture into the center of each, swirling it into the batter with a toothpick to create a cinnamon-raisin-bread effect.

6. Bake for 20–22 minutes, until an inserted toothpick comes out clean. Remove from the oven and allow to slightly cool. Then, while still warm, poke multiple holes into each cupcake. Drizzle around 1 teaspoon of maple syrup on each cupcake to soak through. When cooled, frost each cupcake with vanilla frosting (see recipe, p. 70).

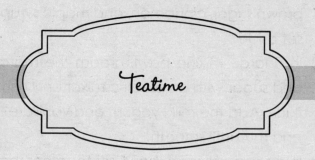

Teatime

"I've been thinking of your cupcakes for days!" Mr. Malik says as he settles onto a chair at the counter. He places a lovely purple orchid on the polished wood. "Phalaenopsis," he says.

"Absolutely lovely," Gran says.

"A thank-you for the last delectable treat." Mr. Malik beams.

I laugh. "For me? Are you jealous, Gran?"

"Oh, pooh." Gran frowns at me, but her eyes twinkle.

"Now tell me," Mr. Malik says, "what is the daily cupcake?"

"French toast."

"Ah! How clever. I'll take that. And my tea, of course."

Gran gathers the loose tea and places it in a pot to brew, and I put one of my latest creations onto a plate.

Mr. Malik looks around, frowning. "Rather busy in here, isn't it?"

He's right; the place is packed — every single table is taken with people chatting or working quietly on computers.

"This is the problem with coffee," Mr. Malik pronounces. "Everyone wants to keep working, keep working. They don't even know what they are drinking! Tea, however — this is to be savored. Isn't that right, Mrs. Wilson?"

"Absolutely, Mr. Malik," Gran agrees. "Savored with good company." She actually makes herself blush when she says this.

"Mother!" Mom comes out of the back office holding an enormous bundle of mail. "Mother — what is all of this?"

Gran bats her eyes innocently. "Mail?"

"Mail! Yes — specifically bills, Mother." Mom dumps the envelopes on the counter. "Some of which are past-due."

"Oh, I never pay attention to those things," Gran says, waving her hand. "I'll just call them up and explain. They always let me pay late."

"Mother, this one says it's *going to a collection agency*." Mom is waving an envelope like it's an exhibit for the prosecution. "That could destroy your credit rating!"

"Well — so?" Gran looks blankly at Mr. Malik, who pours himself a cup of tea.

Mom throws up her hands in frustration. "You're impossible! I'm just going to have to call and sort this out." She stalks off, and I hear her grumbling something about needing a filing cabinet.

"She's turning my hair white," Gran says to Mr. Malik.

"Well, Mrs. Wilson, I think you should consider yourself extremely lucky to have a daughter who wishes to take care of you."

"You're quite correct," Gran says, and takes a sip of her tea.

The bell above the door jingles, and a cold chill falls over the room. The cakes fall flat in the ovens, and the coffee develops frost around the edges. A tumbleweed rolls between the tables.

No, just kidding. It's just Mr. Malik's sister.

Her flashing eyes land on her brother, and he gives her a huge smile. "Ah, Uzma! Just in time to join us in a cup of tea."

"Where did you put the information for tomorrow's orders?" she demands, without acknowledging me or Gran.

"Where they always are."

"I can't find them."

"Well, you'll have to wait. I'm having a cup of tea with my friend Mrs. Wilson."

Uzma glares at Gran. She notices the purple orchid beside the cash register and scowls, as if she wishes she could vaporize it with her eyes. She's never been very happy about Gran and Mr. Malik's barter arrangement. "I need your help now, Umer."

Mr. Malik is unruffled by his sister's temper. "I'll be there in a few minutes."

With a huff, she storms through the door. Mr. Malik smiles gently at Gran, who looks down at her saucer. The happy mood between them has been snuffed out.

It's amazing that one person can have that power.

Confession:
It's My Fault

Once, when I was a little girl, I went into the flower shop with Gran to choose a bouquet for a friend of hers who was in the hospital. Mr. Malik wasn't there for some reason — maybe he was on a delivery — so Uzma was helping Gran. I was bored waiting for Gran to pick out what she wanted, so I made a game of smelling all of the flowers in the shop. I sniffed all of the cut flowers, and then moved on to blooming plants.

Well, one of them had a dead leaf on it, so I picked it off.

Uzma Malik must have caught the movement out of the corner of her eye, because she started screaming at me. She even came out from behind the cash register to scold me, wagging a finger in my face. Naturally, I started to cry, and my grandmother became very stern. She told Ms. Malik that it wasn't her place to speak to a child that way, and that if she had anything to say, she could say it to Gran. Well, Ms. Malik did not like that *at all*. She called Gran an imperialist. That made Gran so mad that she dropped the bouquet on the counter, grabbed my hand, and dragged me out of the store.

When Mr. Malik heard about this incident, he came over with the flowers and an apology, but things have never been the same between Uzma Malik and my grandmother.

All because of a stupid dead leaf.

The Chapter in Which I Wonder Who Is Lying

"*W*here *were* you?"

Artie's voice snaps me out of my thoughts. She's standing on the other side of the counter, her face flushed and happy. "I thought you were going to wait for me!" She's speaking a pitch higher than usual, almost as if someone has turned up the volume on her tongue. I catch sight of the two college guys at the corner table looking over at her, and it strikes me that this is what she wanted. "I got out of the audition and couldn't find you anywhere."

"Sorry — I'm sorry. I just — I realized I had to get back here. I'd told Gran I would help out. . . ." I look over to make sure that Gran is out of earshot. She'd call me on a lie faster than you can smack a bug.

"I went trekking all over school looking for you!"

"Sorry," I repeat. I want to tell her about what happened with Marco, but we're in the middle of the café, and besides . . . "Have a cupcake." I pass it across the counter to her.

"I got the part," Artie announces, beaming.

"That's great!" I rush around the counter and wrap her in a hug. She leans toward me and closes her eyes, still smiling, and — somehow — I get the feeling that we're in a movie, or maybe that Artie thinks we're in a movie. I'm not sure if I'm explaining that right, but it's how I feel. I say, "Congratulations."

"And Devon got his part, too! I'm so glad we got the chance to run lines last Saturday. I think that really made the difference."

"Saturday?"

Artie takes a bite of the cupcake. "Yeah — after I couldn't come over, I called up Devon and asked if he wanted to practice. He only lives about five blocks away — did you know that?"

"You called him?" Why am I turning into a parrot? It's just — I'm feeling all queasy, like that time I jumped on the trampoline after eating three hot dogs. Artie doesn't call guys she hardly knows. She's shy.

Isn't she?

"Yeah. Lucky he was home!" She squeezes my arm. "This is going to be so much fun! Maybe you should help out with the play — you could work on props or wardrobe or something."

I manage to make a vague noise that indicates I'm listening, but I'm not — not really. My head is still processing, the gears grinding slowly. So — Artie spent Saturday with Devon, not me and Marco. And it took her a week to mention it.

Maybe she thought it wasn't a big deal.

Or maybe she thought it *was* a big deal.

Did she really try to get a ride to my house on Saturday?

All of these questions that, for some reason, I just don't dare to ask. Just like I don't dare to tell her about my crush on Devon.

Just like I don't want to talk to her about Marco.

So here's the question: What good is a best friend if you can't tell her anything?

Confession:
Artie Had a Crush on Marco

I shouldn't have said anything.

Artie was sleeping over at my house. It was late — maybe two A.M. — and we were in my room. I was lying in my bed, and she was lying on the trundle. The lights were off, but we were still talking, occasionally drifting off into giggles.

"Can I tell you a secret?" Artie asked.

"Sure." This was a formality. Artie knows that nobody can pry a secret out of me — not even with tweezers.

"I like Marco."

"Muh —" I said. I'd almost said, "Me, too," but stopped myself because I'd realized in that half second what Artie meant, and when I did, my heart started racing.

She propped her head on her elbow. "Don't tease me."

"I won't."

"What do you think — do you think he likes me?"

What did I think? I thought that this conversation was extremely weird. Marco? Artie isn't allowed to have a crush on Marco. He's Marco. Besides . . . what would it mean? How would it — work?

For me, I mean.

"I don't . . . know."

"He's just so cute. Those long eyelashes. And sweet."

"Yeah."

"He has a bad temper, though."

I had nothing to say to that.

"I think he might like me. He was sort of looking at me the other day, and he sat right next to me at lunch."

"Okay."

"You don't think he likes me." I could hear her pout in the darkness.

"I don't know. I just . . ."

"What?"

"Well . . . he's our friend, Artie. What if — what if he doesn't?"

A black wall of silence. "Yeah," she said at last. "I know. Total weirdness."

"I think, maybe, it's a bad idea."

She didn't say anything after that, and I guess we eventually both fell asleep because I woke up a few hours later to sunlight streaming through the window. Artie was already up, the unruly sheets thrust to the side. I could hear her downstairs, chatting with my mom, things clattering in the kitchen.

I sighed and looked up at the blue sky over the side of Marco's house next door. A feeling of dread settled over me, as if I'd narrowly avoided a disaster . . . but only temporarily.

I don't know much about crushes, but in my experience, they're a little hard to control. I hoped Artie would get over hers.

But I don't know if she ever did.

My Top Five Contenders for New School Mascot:

5. The Hissy Fits
4. The Macho Nachos
3. The Zombies
2. The Nefarious Evildoers
1. The Giant Squids

I had to look up what *nefarious* means, which made it even more fun to imagine the cheer squad painting that mascot name on our pep-rally signs.

There are so many cool, creative, original names we could end up with. . . .

"They chose the Eagles," Meghan whispers to me before first period. I'm standing by my locker, trying to rescue a notebook that's buried beneath everything else. It comes loose with a jerk, and I look over at Meghan. Her vibrant purple hair frames her face, and her glasses perch at the tip of her nose. She's wearing some crazy pink, feathered earrings, and basically looks like an exotic parrot. With glasses. This is a look I could never pull off.

"The Eagles?"

"Shh. They aren't announcing it until homeroom." She looks over her shoulder, as if we're discussing state secrets.

"But . . . that's so lame."

"Better than the Purple Pintos," she says.

"Hmm," I say. *Less original than the Purple Pintos*, I think.

"Personally, I have a feeling that the administration rigged the election. But you didn't hear it from me." She pretends to lock her lips and throw away the key.

"Would they do that?"

"Probably not. But it's more fun to think that people voted for the Hissy Fits."

"I know."

Someone taps me on the shoulder, and I turn to see Devon's blue eyes staring down at mine. My heart does a little tap dance and all of the blood in my body rushes to my head at once.

"Hi, Hayley."

He knows my name!

Of course he knows it. We were introduced, weren't we?

But he didn't forget!

Oh, be quiet, brain.

"Hi, Devon."

"Hey, Devon." Meghan gives him a little wave, and her voice sounds about five zillion times more casual than mine. Meghan is one of those people who knows everybody.

I'm looking at those ChapStick-commercial lips, wondering what he'll say. He smiles, and asks, "Do you know where Artemis is?"

My tap-dancing heart stumbles a little, recovers, slows down. "She's, uh . . ." I look over toward Artie's locker, as if she will magically appear. We got off the school bus together, but now she's disappeared. "No. Sorry."

Devon leans against the bank of lockers. "I wanted to tell her about Alex Strasosky's party."

"Everybody's going," Meghan puts in. "You're supposed to dress as whatever mascot you voted for."

"Nobody's going to do that," Devon says.

Meghan shrugs. "Maybe I will."

Devon laughs and looks at me. "You should come, too." Then he walks away, leaving me light as a feather.

"Do you think I should go?" I ask Meghan. "I'm not invited."

"It's not that kind of party," she says. "Everyone's invited. See you in homeroom." Meghan takes off down the hall, and Marco materializes around the corner.

"Hey, Marco!" I call, waving. I walk up to him, and he nods, and then I remember the awkwardness from the day before and feel myself blushing. But now I'm standing in front of him, and what can I do? Run away? "Um . . . there's this party on Saturday at Alex Strasosky's house."

"Okay."

"I thought maybe . . . Everyone's going."

Marco nods again, looks off over his shoulder at nothing in particular. "So — no Game Night?"

"Oh." Game Night. I'd forgotten about it. Now I feel like a jerk for bagging on our usual plan. But — but I know Artie will want to go to the party. "I just . . . uh . . . if you'd rather have Game Night again . . ." I want to catch the words and stuff them back into my mouth. Another Game Night with just Marco will be super awkward.

He looks right into my eyes, and I have the uncomfortable feeling that he's reading my thoughts. "No," he says slowly. "It's cool. Go to the party." He steps around me, like I'm something in the way.

I watch him walk down the hall, wanting to call after him, not daring to call after him. I'm feeling shaky, as if the ground has shifted beneath me, and might suddenly shift again.

Marco is one of my best friends, and suddenly I feel like he hates me.

More Fun with Dad

$\mathcal{D}$ad pulls up to the curb, and I'm starting to follow Chloe into the backseat when I realize that the front passenger seat is empty.

"No Annie?" I ask, maybe a little too happily.

"She's meeting us at the restaurant."

Great. I nod grimly and climb in beside my dad, balancing the white bakery box on my lap.

Chloe chatters happily about Rupert as I look out the window. I can see my grandmother behind the counter inside the tea shop. She waves to us as Dad pulls away from the curb, and I wave back, even though the windows are tinted and I know she can't see me.

Dad makes a left turn at the light. Our usual pizza parlor is to the right. "Where are we going?"

"I thought we'd try a new place."

"Why?" I ask, which is a little babyish, since I know why. We're going to a new place because of Annie, who is too good for pizza, obviously.

"It's good to try new things." Dad's voice is strained, but he tries hard to make it sound relaxed.

"Where?" Chloe asks.

"Rain."

I haven't even heard of it, but I can tell it's fancy the moment Dad pulls into the parking lot. The lettering on the sign is gold and hard to read. Inside, the lighting is dim and the walls are hung with plush red curtains. Candles give everything a soft yellow glow.

"A waterfall!" Chloe says, and Dad laughs.

She's right. Near the windows is a whole wall of rocks with water cascading down, collecting in a stone pool.

Annie is already there, sitting at a table by herself. She waves to us and Dad waves back. Chloe hurries over to join her.

"Hi, Hayley!" Annie says brightly when she sees me, like we're old friends.

"Hi."

Dad bends over and gives Annie a quick kiss, then takes the chair beside her. Sitting across from them, I can see that they aren't as strange a couple as I first thought. My dad's hair is dark and graying slightly at the temples, which makes his blue eyes seem bright. He's wearing a purple button-down shirt and dark jeans that look new, and I wonder if Annie helped him pick them out. Anyway, the clothes make him look younger, and I realize suddenly that my dad is handsome. I guess I've never thought about it before. He's handsome and young-looking, and now he has this pretty, young girlfriend, and I can't help feeling like he's someone I've never met.

"So, what would you girls like to drink?" Dad asks, once the waitress has handed us our menus.

"Ginger ale," Chloe says, fast as a bullet.

"I'll take the dollar," I say.

Annie lifts her eyebrows and looks at my dad, who turns red and starts to dig in his back pocket for his wallet. Two years ago, my dad offered me and Chloe a deal — every time we skip ordering drinks in a restaurant, we get a dollar. It's supposed to teach us about saving money or something, but a dollar is usually less than what a drink costs, so he comes out ahead. It's funny — Dad doesn't mind spending money on stuff that looks good, like a fancy apartment or a nice car. But when it comes to paying for a soda or a bottle of water, forget it.

"Spend it wisely," Dad says when he hands over the dollar. It's what he always says.

"I will." I always spend my money on cupcake ingredients, which I think is at least borderline wise.

"What's in there?" Annie eyes the white box that I've propped on my plate. I fiddle with the red-and-white bakery string.

"Cupcakes. I thought we could have them for dessert."

"Ooh, I love cupcakes!"

"She made them," Chloe pipes up.

"You made them? Let's see." Annie peers over the table curiously.

I hesitate a moment, but finally pull the string. I lift the lid and tilt the box toward Annie. The dim candlelight makes her eyes glow as she takes a look at the cupcakes.

"Beautiful," she breathes. "What flavor?"

"Gingered pumpkin," I say. "With chocolate frosting."

"Sounds fantastic." My dad smiles. "You're really improving."

I'm really improving. It's true — the frosting is even and I put a light touch of colored sugar on top to give it some sparkle. Still, the comment bugs me. I know he means it as a compliment, but it sounds like he thinks I'm a kid trying to learn how to roller-skate.

Annie is still looking down at the cupcakes. "Where did you get the recipe?"

"I made it up."

"She makes the *best* cupcakes," Chloe gushes, and I want to hug her.

Annie looks at me, thoughtful. "I've never baked anything," she says. "Unless you can make it from a mix." She laughs a little, and I close the box and tie it up.

"Annie has something for you girls," Dad announces. Annie looks a little embarrassed, but reaches for a small shopping bag hooked onto her chair.

"It's nothing. Just —" She hands over two small packages, one for Chloe, one for me. Naturally, Chloe rips hers open in less than half a second.

"Oh, *thank* you!" she exclaims when she sees the black notebook and colored pencils. "I love drawing!"

"It's nothing," Annie says again, waving her hand, but she smiles, clearly pleased.

Chloe immediately spills the pencils out of their decorative tin case, running her fingers over the beautiful colors. They're slim and elegant, and it looks like Annie bought them in a real art store. I wonder how she knew that my sister loved drawing. *I* didn't even really know . . . not until that very minute, when Chloe said so.

"Open yours, Hayley," Dad says.

"It's just a token," Annie puts in.

I can tell by the shape that it's a book, and I'm not surprised to see pages when I tear off the corner. But I am surprised by the title: *Amber Violetta, Teen Star! Totally Unauthorized Biography!*

Wow.

Amber Violetta.

I really hate her music.

"Thank you," I say.

"I was always reading books about pop stars when I was your age," Annie spews. "Of course, they were all Thai! But I really loved to know all about them."

"This is great." I'm a liar, but what else can I say?

"Annie picked it out especially for you." Dad's eyes are heavy with meaning.

"Thanks so much," I repeat, failing to make it sound like this is The Present I've Been Dying for My Entire Life.

"It's nothing," Annie says, and then thank goodness the waitress comes over to take our order. I stash the book and the box beneath my seat.

Dad has to help Chloe with the menu — lots of the words are in French — and Annie and I lock eyes briefly over the candle flame. She smiles, but it's an expression that seems almost like an apology. I look away.

She knows I hate the book.

And Then I Went to
Alex's Party

It only takes about thirty seconds for me to regret coming to Alex's party. It's packed — I guess the whole school found out about it — and loud. Music is blaring in the enormous living room, echoing off the cathedral ceilings, and a bunch of kids are crammed around the snack table in the dining room, off to the right. Nobody is dressed as their favorite mascot, but a lot of the girls seem like they're dressed up. I'm seeing a few dresses, a couple of sequined tank tops. Everyone's hair looks done. I feel suddenly self-conscious in my T-shirt and jeans.

"Do I look okay?" I ask Artie.

She shrugs. "You look fine."

Fine. Not the reassurance I was hoping for. Artie, on the other hand, looks fantastic. She's wearing a flowered tunic over a pair of leggings, and her hair falls in loose waves around her face.

Why didn't I ask what she was wearing? I wonder, feeling like the nerdy younger sister dragged along to a high school party. And, at the same time, I wonder why Artie didn't tell me that she was going to get dressed up. By the time Mom and I picked her up to take her to the party, it was too late for me to change.

Chang waves from the middle of the living room. Artie rushes over to her, plunging into the thick of the pulsing dance floor. I hang back. I don't feel like having a shouted non-conversation with Chang and Artie, and I don't want to just follow my best friend around all night.

But I can't just stand in the front foyer, either, so I head in the other direction — to the snack table. I say hey to Ellie Fisk and LaShonda Joyner and survey the snacks. There's nothing that really interests me — everything looks like it just came out of a bag. I'm debating whether or not to take a handful of chips when someone hovers at my shoulder.

"Is there something to drink over here?" Kyle Kempner smiles at me, and I wonder if he even realizes who I am, or if I'm just a giant blur to him.

"Yeah, punch," I say. It's neon pink and looks like it might be radioactive, and I wonder if I should warn him. I guess all punch looks like this. "Want me to get some for you?"

"Oh, Fred!" He smiles, recognizing my voice. "That

would be great." His blond hair is spiked out in crazy pyramids, and he's dressed all in black.

I'm wondering if he's gone punk, which would be kind of weird, but actually looks good on him. "I like your hair."

"I'm dressed as a Hissy Fit," he says. "That's what I voted for."

"Oh, I get it."

I hand him the drink, and he says, "Thanks. Nobody else is dressed up, are they?"

"Not exactly," I admit, feeling a little bad for him.

"I knew they wouldn't. People are so lame."

"I'm wearing a shirt with an octopus on it," I say. "I voted for the Giant Squids."

"And that, Hayley, is why you are the coolest girl at Adams." He takes a sip of his neon-pink punch and smiles at me.

Someone thinks I'm the coolest girl at Adams? I'm so surprised that I can't even think of a response.

Marco appears at that moment, and I give him a huge smile, but he barely nods at me. "Hey, Kyle." Marco puts a hand on his shoulder. "Pete is looking for you."

"Where is he?"

"Sitting at the bottom of the stairs. Turn right as you walk out of this room. Need me to take you?"

"I've got it. Great talking to you, Hayley." Kyle smiles and takes off, and I'm impressed at how easily he navigates his way through the crowded room.

Marco and I are left staring at each other. "I didn't know you were going to come," I say.

Marco shrugs and looks over my head. "Didn't have anything else to do."

That stings, and suddenly I'm dying for a change of subject. "Chloe and I had dinner with Dad and Annie tonight."

Marco looks down at me, his dark eyes softening a bit. "How did it go?"

"She gave me a biography of Amber Violetta."

"She called that one wrong."

"I know."

"At least she's trying."

I sigh.

"Too bad people can't be exactly how you want them to be, Hayley," Marco says, and walks away.

I stare after him, trying to figure out what he meant. "How *do* I want them to be?" I ask the empty air.

"How do you want what to be?" Meghan asks, smiling, as if I'm about to tell her a joke. She's sneaked up on me, which isn't hard, given that the volume in this room is deafening.

"Oh, nothing. It was just a . . ." I glance after Marco,

who's talking to a bunch of his guy friends in the next room. Ignoring me.

"Random thought?"

"Yeah."

I'm really liking Meghan's look. She's wearing a black dress and pink-and-black striped tights with chunky Mary Janes. She points to my shirt. "Did you vote for the Squids?"

"Yep."

"Awesome!"

"Too bad we lost."

"I feel like I won. We got rid of the Pintos."

"Thanks to you."

"Meh." One shoulder rises, then dips. "It's something everyone had complained about for years. I'm just the one who made up a petition. So, what's the matter — you don't dance?" She nods toward the living room.

I look out at the mass of people moving to the beat, and suddenly feel sick. There. Right there, in the corner. It's Devon. He's talking to a girl, his hand pressed against the wall behind her, his face close to hers. She laughs at something he says, and when he moves slightly to the right, I realize that the girl is Artie.

"Hey," Meghan says after a moment. She puts a gentle hand on my arm. "Hey, are you okay? You look kind of . . ."

"Fine." But my voice is a whisper, like a ghost of my real voice.

"You don't look fine. Let's go outside." I look at her face, and her eyes are honest, concerned. "You need some air."

And I'm suddenly glad that Meghan is a little bossy, because she takes my arm and guides me out through the back door, which is just what I needed, but didn't know it. Then I'm standing on the deck, blinking back tears and trying to clear my hot, fuzzy throat, but the cool air feels good.

There are a few kids in the backyard, talking. Meghan steers me away from them, down the long asphalt driveway. Alex's house is in a development on the edge of nowhere, bordered by forest. I had noticed the darkness growing as Mom drove farther and farther from Northampton. There's only one streetlamp on his block, and as Meghan and I start up the sidewalk, I wonder if a bear might lumber across our path. *When do they sleep?* I wonder. *Aside from all winter.* My mind shifts from sadness to fear with only a slight click, like a dial being turned.

"Look at all the stars," Meghan says, and when I follow her gaze, I realize that she's right. So many stars, and they look larger than they do at home. The moon, too, is full, and after a minute, my eyes have adjusted and I realize that it's not as dark as I thought.

"Isn't it amazing to think about how old they are?" Meghan's face is turned toward the sky, her long neck creating a graceful curve in the darkness. "It takes the light millions of years to reach us. Some of these stars haven't existed for centuries, but we can still see them."

"Like ghosts."

"Only their light is real. Real for us."

"But that's what a ghost is, right? Something that's still real for whoever's seeing it. Even if it doesn't exist anymore."

She turns to me. "You're deep, Hayley."

"I'm not trying to be."

Some of the houses are lit up, and I can see inside. Empty rooms or families gathered around the TV sets. "I have a crush on this guy." I don't know what makes me say this, but it comes out in a rush.

Meghan waits for me to go on.

"It's Devon. I never told Artie about it, and now . . ."

". . . maybe it's too late," Meghan finishes.

"Yeah."

"You think she likes him?"

"I don't know. But I think he likes her, so I'm not sure it matters." I think about Devon leaning close to Artie, her face turned to his, and wonder if I'm a liar.

"That's . . . bad." We start around the curve of the

cul-de-sac, which will eventually lead us right back where we started. "But Artie is your best friend, right?"

"Of course."

"So — what can you do?"

Exactly. "How's Ben?"

"You remembered!" She laughs, clearly delighted to talk about her own crush. "He's at home. His parents never let him come to parties."

"What is it that you like about him?"

"Oh." She bends to pick up a twig. "Remember that trip to the planetarium? He sat next to me." She breaks the stick in half, tosses it away. "He's so interesting. He's" — she shakes her head — "different. We were talking about the universe, and God, and . . . So — why do you like Devon?"

"He almost helped me pick up my books once."

Meghan laughs, a sound like a silver bell, and I realize how dumb I must sound. But she doesn't tease me. Instead she says, "Sweet guy."

"That's what I thought."

We've arrived at Alex's house again, which shines brilliantly in the darkness. Movement and noise flow from the building like a pulse. "Do you want to go back inside?" Meghan asks.

"No."

"Should we walk more?"

I think about the possibility of bears and decide the party is worse right now. "Do you mind?"

"I'd love it," Meghan says, and her smile tells me that she means it.

So we walk back into the dark night, letting the noise of the party fade behind us.

Heartsick Puppies
(makes approximately 12 cupcakes)

These cupcakes are based on my Omi's stollen recipe, which she would make for breakfast year-round. She was a great baker, just like Gran. I used pine nuts, because I was thinking of my old house on Pine Street, I guess, and the way that Artie and I used to be so close . . . right in each other's backyards. I wonder if I would have told her about my crush if I still lived there. Maybe.

Maybe.

INGREDIENTS:
- 1 cup milk
- 1 teaspoon apple cider vinegar
- 1 cup plus 2 tablespoons all-purpose flour
- 1 teaspoon baking powder
- 1/4 teaspoon baking soda
- 1/2 teaspoon salt
- 2/3 cup sugar
- 1/4 teaspoon vanilla extract
- 1/2 teaspoon almond extract
- 1/3 cup canola oil

1/3 cup pine nuts, finely ground (just put them in the blender or food processor)

1/4 cup chopped pine nuts

1/2 cup minced candied citrus peel (orange and lemon)

INSTRUCTIONS:

1. Preheat the oven to 350°F. Line a muffin pan with cupcake liners.
2. Whisk the milk and vinegar in a small bowl, and set aside for a few minutes to get good and curdled.
3. In a large bowl, sift together the flour, baking powder, baking soda, and salt, and mix.
4. In a separate large bowl, mix the curdled milk with the sugar.
5. Add in the vanilla extract, almond extract, oil, and ground pine nuts. Then, blend with a whisk or handheld mixer. Add the dry ingredients a little bit at a time, stopping occasionally to scrape the sides of the bowl, and mix until no lumps remain.
6. Fold in the chopped pine nuts and candied citrus peel.

7. Fill cupcake liners two-thirds of the way and bake for 20–22 minutes. Transfer to a cooling rack, and let cool completely before frosting with vanilla frosting (see recipe, p. 70).

More Cupcakes for Breakfast

$\mathcal{I}$ walk into homeroom and place the tray of cupcakes on Ms. Anderson's desk. "Is this okay?" I ask.

She barely looks up from her paperwork. "Did you bring one for me?"

"I brought one for everyone."

"Then it's fine," she says. "You can place mine right here." She indicates a spot away from her papers. Ms. Anderson stands up. "Everyone, take your seats. As you can see, we have some treats here, courtesy of Hayley. Anyone who wants one can come up in an orderly fashion —"

She can't even finish the sentence. Chairs scrape the floors as everyone dashes to the front of the room. "I said orderly!" Ms. Anderson insists. "Is this orderly?" But no one is listening. It reminds me of the time Chloe and I went to see a piranha feeding at the aquarium — all crazy movement and gobbling.

"I love cupcakes for breakfast!" Raviv Godhi takes a huge bite and grins at me with a gooey smile.

"What flavor is it?" Chang asks.

"Stollen — it's this German Christmas cake. . . ."

"You're a demented genius!"

Artie grins. "Hayley has a way with a cupcake."

I smile at her, but it feels tight, like I've pulled a muscle in my face. After Meghan and I went back to the party, I found Artie. Devon had gone off somewhere, thank goodness. Anyway, I told Artie that I didn't feel well and thought I would go home. And she just said, "Okay, I'll get a ride home with Chang or Devon," and I felt like a popped balloon and haven't felt right since.

Even working on the cupcakes yesterday felt off. Measuring and mixing, baking and frosting. These things can usually absorb my whole attention. But yesterday, I found my mind kept wandering off, thinking about Artie and Devon, wondering what would happen if they became a couple, imagining my lonely lunches and empty weekends. So when the cupcakes came out and I frosted the tops and sprinkled them with chopped pine nuts, I decided to call them Heartsick Puppies, since I felt like I'd stirred my sad, confused feelings about Artie and Devon right into the batter.

The worst part? I couldn't even talk to my best friend about it.

And speaking of friends . . . I notice Meghan is the only person still in her seat, reading her book, as if there isn't a crazy cupcake party happening at the front of the room.

"Hey, Meghan," I say, coming over to her desk. "Do you want a cupcake? There's a couple left." I hold one out to her. It's particularly gooey, covered in thick frosting.

Meghan puts down her book. "I'm allergic to gluten."

"To what?"

"Gluten. It's a protein in wheat and some other grains." She says this as if she's had to explain it a thousand times before.

"So — you can't have bread?"

"Bread, pizza, cupcakes, muffins, pasta — whatever." Meghan shrugs. "Unless it's gluten free, like made with rice flour or something."

I look down at the cupcake. "Sorry."

"I'm used to it."

Raviv overhears us and starts making a loud yummy noise. "Mmmm! Meghan, this is so good! So much delicious gluten!"

I look down at Meghan. "Are you used to that?" I ask.

She rolls her eyes. "Yep."

I sit down in the chair beside hers. "It must be hard to watch other people eating."

"It isn't really — I mean, I know that if I eat a cupcake, I'll puke or get sick, so I don't want it so much."

"I think I would die without cupcakes," I say.

"I can still have cupcakes. They just have to be gluten free. And you really wouldn't die. You'd miss them, that's all. Then you'd get over it."

I look down at the cupcake in my hand. I know I wouldn't really die without it. I prefer baking cupcakes to eating them, anyway. But it just seems so unfair.

I feel really bad for bringing the cupcakes in, but Meghan clearly isn't thinking about them — she's gone back to reading her book.

At the front of the classroom, the cupcakes have disappeared. A few stray crumbs on my tray and a wastebasket stuffed with cupcake wrappers are the only signs that they were ever there. The only one left is the one in my hand.

I look at my classmates — Raviv licking his lips, Artie and Chang giggling. I wonder if any of them would be as cool as Meghan if they had to give up eating wheat.

It's not the food that would bother me, I decide. *It's the being different.*

Meghan Markerson is different.

Not everyone can handle that.

The Right Kind of Friend

It's quiet in the café, and the afternoon sunlight slants in, covering the floor in gold. Three tables are taken. One by the raggedy-looking college student who brought his housemates the bacon cupcakes. He's become a regular — Jerome — and he's fun to chat with, but right now he's reading a thick volume of something that looks like it would put me to sleep in about five minutes. Chloe and Rupert are at the table by the window, both reading. Gran and Mr. Malik are across from each other in the far corner, chatting quietly and sipping tea. I can hear the *click* and *tap* of my keyboard as I look up information about gluten-free recipes. The silence is a little unnerving.

I clear my throat, just to hear something. Then I start humming as I pull up a page with a few GF chocolate cupcakes. GF, by the way, stands for *gluten free*. It turns out that loads of people have a gluten allergy, and they're all online, yakking about food.

Anyway, I open this page, and some sound track comes blaring out so loudly that I jump about a foot in the air. I hit the MUTE button, but Chloe is already glaring at me from across the room. She shushes me.

"Don't you guys want to go outside and play, or something?" I ask. I look out the window, at the blue sky and puffy white clouds. Rupert hasn't even glanced up from his book. "Go have some fun," I suggest.

"We are having fun. Right, Rupert?"

No response.

"Rupert!" She gives him a little kick under the chair.

"Hmm?" He looks up, blinking at her from behind his thick glasses.

"Aren't we having fun?"

Rupert stares at my sister for a moment, as if he's trying to remember who she is, or maybe what planet she's from. "Of course."

"There — see?"

"What time is it?" Rupert asks, looking up at the clock on the wall. "Oh, no. I was supposed to be home ten minutes ago." He shoves his book into his bag and stands up.

"See you tomorrow." Chloe waves as he heads out the

door, then passes by the window. "What?" she asks, looking at me.

I shut my computer and walk over to her table. I hold her eyes as I sit down across from her. "Do you ever wish Rupert would talk more?"

"Why would I want him to talk more?"

"Don't you wish he were more interesting?"

"He's one of the most interesting people I've ever met."

"But he doesn't —"

"Hayley, maybe you don't want to give people a chance, but I do, okay?" She grabs her bag and hurries through the back door.

I feel my grandmother's eyes on me. I know I must be looking guilty, because that's how I'm feeling.

"What just happened?" she asks.

"Um."

"What did you say to your sister?"

"Nothing! I just asked if she ever wished Rupert would talk more."

My grandmother and Mr. Malik exchange a glance. "And what did she say?" Gran asks.

"She said no."

"But you don't believe her." Mr. Malik gives me a kind smile.

"Well . . . I mean, they just sit here and read! Does that seem normal to you?"

"Normal?" Mr. Malik and Gran exchange another look, and this time she suppresses a small smile.

I'm getting really exasperated. "Shouldn't they be doing something?"

"Reading is doing something," Mr. Malik says.

Gran nods. "Reading is one of life's great pleasures."

Oh, boy.

"A good book is the precious lifeblood of a master spirit." Mr. Malik smiles into his tea.

"John Milton?" Gran asks. "Oh, how delightful. You know, I haven't read *Paradise Lost* since —"

And they're off, talking about books. I should have known better than to try to get them to worry about Chloe and Rupert. I'm sure my grandmother thinks it's adorable that they like to read together.

But I can't help thinking that maybe Chloe could do better — get a friend who's livelier. I wonder if she misses her old friends. She never talks about them.

I wonder if they ever think about her.

From the Phone Files: Part 2

"Hey, Artie, can I come over?"

"What? Hold on, sorry, Roan is trying to tell me something. (Yes. Yes. I don't care. No, I'll be here tonight. What's Myla doing? She is?) Okay. Hi, I'm back."

"What's Myla doing?"

"Going to the library to study for the U.S. Government AP exam."

"What's Roan doing?"

"Baseball something. He wants me to work the concession stand, which I'm not doing. You're so lucky you don't have older siblings."

"So — can I come over?"

"Um, sure. Why?"

"I want to bake some cupcakes."

Artie laughs.

"No, really. But they have to be gluten free. I talked to this guy at the health-food store, and he said that if I'm baking in a place where flour is flying all around, they could get cross-contaminated."

"So?"

"So — that's enough to make Meghan sick. All it takes is a tiny bit. Obviously, there's flour all over the bakery. And Mom is using our tiny kitchen to make dinner."

"Why are you making Meghan a gluten-free cupcake?"

"I just — I felt bad that she couldn't have a cupcake today."

"What's the big deal?"

Silence. "So — you don't want me to come over?"

"Whatever; it's fine. I just don't know why you're doing it. It seems like a pain."

"It's no big deal. You just use different kinds of flour, like rice instead of wheat. Did you know that there's chickpea flour?"

"I'll probably have to run lines while you're over. We're supposed to be off-book in two weeks."

"What does off-book mean?"

"It means you have your part memorized."

"It's no big deal, Artie. I just want to use your kitchen. You don't have to entertain me."

"It's just . . . Okay."

"I can come?"

"Sure, come over."

"See you."

"Bye."

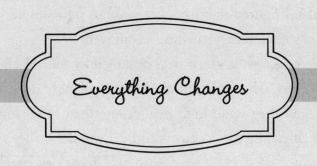

Everything Changes

A light film of grime covers the bus window, blurring the view of familiar houses as we rumble down streets I've known all my life. Taking the city bus is a new experience for me, and a bit disconcerting. It's like having my mother drive me somewhere, only at a much slower pace and much higher up off the ground. I'm surprised at how drab the houses look to me as we head out of downtown. The streets are almost empty. Now that we live in the center of Northampton, I'm used to seeing people — moms with strollers, cool college students, professor types, street musicians. Out here, the place looks a little . . . blank.

The bus is half-empty, and a paper shopping bag occupies the seat beside mine. It contains tapioca starch, potato starch, rice flour, cocoa, sugar, eggs, xanthan gum — all the ingredients you need to make a gluten-free chocolate cupcake. I figured that it makes sense to start simple. I can get fancy later, if this batch turns out well.

We pass a wide green field occupied by four black-and-white cows. The agricultural high school next door raises them, and they stand in a small group, their heads lowered to the emerald grass, as cars whiz by. I wonder if they all get along, or if they ever have cow spats. Do they ever feel sad? Lonely? Happy?

It's hard to tell from a distance, behind a blurry window.

We turn up the street and pass Cooper's Corner, the convenience store I used to walk to whenever we needed something — some bananas, say, or ice cream. I press the button and the bus comes to a stop.

My old house is about three blocks from here, and I enjoy seeing the leaves changing colors in everyone's yard as I walk. The yellow house on the corner's maple is turning a cheery orange. Across the street, the purple Japanese maple is starting to lose its leaves. The red house four doors down has maroon mums and laid-out cedar bark, and the recent rain releases the smell. Each house, each yard, is as familiar to me as my own body, and it feels good to see them again.

I should turn at the next street — Artie's street — but I decide to go past my old house first. I turn down my ex-street (my *ex-street*? Is that a word? But that's what it is . . .)

and climb the hill, cradling my bag in my arms. Even the strain in my muscles feels good and familiar. I'd thought that it might make me sad to see my old house again, but instead, what I feel is a thrill. There's a red jogging stroller on the front porch, and someone has hung a yellow, plastic toddler swing from the tree. I hadn't realized that a family had moved into our house. I wonder if the baby has my old room.

And there, right beside my old house, is Marco. He's turning the soil in his family's flower bed, and I know instantly how much money he is making for this chore, and the fact that his older sister has refused to help, and that — secretly — he would do it for free, because he loves working in the garden. I know these things because they're always the same, and it makes me so thrilled to know them that I shout, "Marco!" and my voice sounds so loud and so happy that I almost don't recognize it.

He looks up and smiles, like he's surprised and happy, and I quicken my step. But then his face clouds over and he glances toward the front door, like he's considering making an escape. It's too late, though. I can't turn back, either, so my feet propel me forward, and soon we're facing each other, separated only by a paper shopping bag and a hoe and about a zillion miles.

"Hi," he says.

"Hi."

"What are you doing here?"

"I'm heading over to Artie's."

"Ah."

"Yeah. I see some new people have moved into our house."

"Do you know anything about them? We're trying to figure them out. They drive a Saab."

"What does that mean?"

"Nobody knows."

"No — I don't know anything."

"They seem nice."

"Good." I want to say that I hope the baby is cute, that I hope it likes my room, but my discomfort keeps my lips sewn shut. I shift my weight from one foot to the other. "Are you — are we doing Game Night this week?"

He looks at the ground, digging in the dirt half-heartedly with his hoe. A clump of dirt lands on a yellow mum flower, burying the bloom in a mudslide. "Look, Hayley — I think . . ." He shakes his head, like he needs help to get a thought out. "I think we really shouldn't hang out. Anymore." He meets my eyes. "As much."

"What?" I feel like someone has stepped on me with a

giant shoe — like I've been crushed, and splattered across the sole. "Why?"

"I don't want — people might get the wrong idea."

"Nobody has the wrong idea." My words are a whisper, but it's so quiet out here that it's impossible to miss them.

And the look he gives me then — it's like the shoe has crushed *him* now. He shakes his head and looks over at his front door. "I've got to go." He walks away from me then, and I want to call after him, but I have no breath. All of the air has been squeezed out of me and a heavy weight has settled on my shoulders, and I feel so much as if I've turned to stone that I wonder if my heart is still beating.

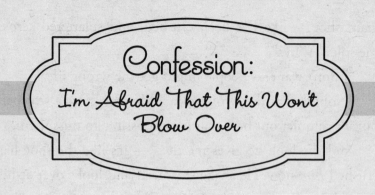

Confession:
I'm Afraid That This Won't Blow Over

$\mathcal{M}$arco never speaks to Sanjit Patel. Never. Last year, they were partnered on a science project. Marco asked Mr. Forbes for a reassignment, but Mr. Forbes is a notorious jerk and refused. Okay, so I was sure that Marco would finally, finally talk to Sanjit rather than get an F on the project. But no. They completed their assignment entirely over e-mail.

Sanjit is a nice guy with a wide smile and a good sense of humor. So what's the problem?

In fourth grade, Sanjit made fun of Marco's sister. She has autism, and doesn't really talk. She was in fifth grade then, and went to a special school, but she had come to our school carnival the week before. I remember. One minute, Sarah was watching a game of musical chairs. Five kids circled around and around four empty chairs while music played. The music stopped, the kids all ran for the chairs.

Sarah let out a shout, then hit herself on the head, over and over. Lots of kids were scared, and Marco's family had to leave.

I remember Marco's face. His skin burned red, but not with embarrassment. His dark eyes flashed and he held his head high, as if he were daring anyone to say something. Nobody did.

Nobody did, until the following Monday. At lunch, Sanjit sat down beside Marco, and out of the blue, he let out a yell and started hitting himself on the head. Dark veins stood out on Marco's neck, and he shouted at Sanjit. Then he took a fistful of mashed potato and threw it at him, and who knows what would have happened if Ms. Nauman and Mr. Witt hadn't come over and separated them.

I haven't thought about that day in a long time. Years, maybe.

We all know that Marco has a temper, but as Sanjit can tell you, he also holds a grudge. He holds it, and never lets it go.

The Things I Do Not Say

I walk on, around the corner, instead of cutting through my ex-backyard, like I usually would. The air has been heavy with cool mist, but the sun peeks out, filtering through the pines that border Artie's family's property. My conversation with Marco burns in my chest like a half-digested meal as I knock on the side door. Her brother, Roan, answers. He doesn't even say hi, he just looks at me, then turns and shouts, "Artemis!" then strolls off. I guess I should be flattered that he treats me like a sister, but I still think it's rude.

The television has been blaring in the other room, but it cuts off suddenly and a moment later, Artie appears in the kitchen as I dump my bag on the breakfast table.

"Hey, you're here."

"Hi. I ran into Marco on the way over."

"Oh, yeah?"

I can taste the words in my mouth, and I'm about to say them — to tell her all about Marco — because even though I know it will be a little awkward, given her past crush and all, I have to talk to someone, and who else is there? So I open my mouth, and at that moment, Devon walks in from the living room, like he has some kind of right to be there.

"Hi, Hayley." He's holding a blue bowl, and turns to Artie. "Is there any more ice cream?"

"In the freezer." Artie smiles at me. "We're watching the movie version."

"Of what — your play?"

Artie nods. "Ms. Lang said we should."

"It's brilliant," Devon says as he scoops something chocolatey into his bowl. "I just wish I could do an accent like that guy."

"You don't really need to," Artie tells him.

There is a sliding door that leads to a patio, and as I look out, the sun dims a bit. The clouds have returned, and the brief light fades behind a wall of dreary gray that mutes everything, even the colors of the grass and the red fire bushes. "Don't mind me," I say. "You guys should go back to your movie. I'll just be in the kitchen."

"You sure?" Artie asks, and Devon says, "Okay." He heads back into the living room, but Artie lingers a moment, like she can see that something's wrong. And for a moment I think, *I will tell her.*

But then Devon calls, "Artemis!" and I feel like the mum bent beneath the weight of a clump of dirt, extinguished.

Artie shrugs. "I've got to —"

"Okay."

She leaves, and I get to work on the cupcakes. It isn't hard. I know her kitchen as well as my own, and better than I know Gran's. I can see into the living room from where I stand, mixing the batter. Artie and Devon have their backs to me. Devon's arm is stretched along the top of the couch, almost as if it is around Artie.

I pour the batter into the cupcake wrappers in silence. I wash up as they bake, then sit and stare into the fading light as the cocoa smell begins to waft through the house. After eighteen minutes, I test the cupcakes. They are firm, so I place them carefully into my cupcake carrier. I put two on the counter. I'll frost the others at home.

Then, without a word, I leave out the side door.

Cupcakes Are a Serious Issue

I t takes me forty minutes to get home, and it's dark by the time I walk through the door. Mom is on the phone, and she frowns at my cupcakes as she says, "Yes. Yes, I'll be there."

I step into Gran's tiny kitchen and unpack my bag. There's a reason I didn't want to bake the cupcakes here. Downstairs, it's flour city. Upstairs, the kitchen is so small that it can barely hold two people, and Mom has something simmering on the stove and a half-made salad on the counter.

"Hullo, darling!" Gran chirps from the dining room. She and Chloe are setting the table. "How is Artie?"

"Fine," I say just as Mom clicks off.

"You will not believe who that was. It was Juliet Markerson."

"Why?" I ask. Juliet Markerson — Meghan's mother. I

wonder if Meghan is inviting me to a party, but my mother's tense face suggests it's something else.

"Because I'm on the PTO, and she's the president, and she has decided that she wants to ban cupcakes at Adams."

"What?" It's half word, half gasp.

"That's silly." Gran waves her hand, as if she can't bear to listen to such stupidity.

"Why?" Chloe asks.

"It's an obesity issue, she says. And a food-allergy issue. She says that you can never be sure about the sanitary conditions in an individual's home. So — no more bake sales, no more birthday celebrations, nothing like that." My mother huffs and sits down at the table, eyeing my cupcake carrier.

"That's absurd. What about common sense?" Gran demands. "Overweight children aren't overweight because they buy a cupcake at a bake sale."

"I know, Mother, but — on the other hand — how necessary are cupcakes?" Mom asks. "I mean, the athletic teams could sell something else to raise money."

"But a bake sale is something that everyone can help with," Chloe points out.

"Well, anyway, Hayley, I hope you weren't planning on bringing these into school tomorrow." Mom taps her fingernails on the carrier's plastic cover.

The whole time everyone has been talking, I've been feeling like a boa constrictor has wrapped itself around me and is busy squeezing, flexing its muscles until my whole body aches. But when Mom looks up at me, I feel the heat and pain pour out through my eyes, and hot tears spill down my cheeks.

"Hayley, honey!" Mom jumps up and wraps me in a hug, pressing me against her soft body. Her sweatshirt smells like our fabric softener. "What's wrong?" She pulls away to look into my face.

"It's not that." I brush the tears away, embarrassed that I'm overreacting. "It's just — I've had a bad day." I give a little hiccup.

"They're just cupcakes, Hayley," Chloe says, looking worried.

Mom pushes the hair away from my face. "Did you — did you want to take these in tomorrow?"

"Just one." I smile weakly. "It's gluten free. For Meghan Markerson."

"Oh," Mom says, looking confused.

"This is my fault. I brought in cupcakes this morning, and Meghan couldn't have one because she's allergic."

"Sweetheart." Mom hugs me again.

"Well, I can't believe her mother would spoil things for

everyone just because her own daughter has an allergy." Gran is sputtering, as if the entire thought is an insult.

"But that's no reason to cry, is it?" Mom looks at me, clearly worried. I know what she's thinking: *It's the divorce, it's the move, it's my job.* But it doesn't have anything to do with her.

"No." I take a deep breath. "It's no reason to cry." *Just because I'm losing everything.*

"Should we try one?" Mom asks.

"Before supper?" Gran is scandalized, but Mom silences her with a look.

"Sure," I say, and I pop open the carrier. Everyone takes one, even Gran. I'm not sure what to expect, but when I bite into the cupcake, it's moist and still slightly warm. The texture is just right — not too dense, which was what I was afraid of. And the cocoa shines through, sweet and soothing.

"Yum!" Chloe says, and Gran agrees.

"Delicious," she proclaims.

Mom takes a deep breath, and puts her half-eaten cupcake down on the counter. "Sweetie, the meeting isn't until Wednesday. I think you can still take a cupcake to school, if you want."

"Really?"

Mom smiles. "They haven't been banned yet. And they may not be. Juliet may not get the votes."

I'm relieved. I really want Meghan to have a cupcake, to make up for the ones she couldn't have today. "These would be good with chocolate frosting."

"I'll help," Chloe volunteers.

"After supper." Gran's voice is firm.

So we clean up and I pour water into everyone's cup, and then we sit down to dinner, just like we always do. My tears have dried up, and I feel like an empty husk, fragile but clean. Darkness has settled over everything outside, but the moon is rising. It looks enormous and orange from the window, and I'm glad to see it.

Gluten-Free Chocolate Cupcakes
(makes approximately 12–15 cupcakes)

These are really good. You won't miss the gluten, believe me.

INGREDIENTS:
- 1/2 cup milk
- 1/2 teaspoon vinegar
- 1 cup plus 1 tablespoon gluten-free all-purpose flour (I made my own, but you can use Bob's Red Mill.)
- 1/4 cup cocoa powder, unsweetened
- 1/2 teaspoon baking powder
- 3/4 teaspoon baking soda
- 1/4 teaspoon salt
- 1/2 cup semisweet chocolate chips
- 3/4 cup sugar
- 1 teaspoon vanilla extract
- 1/4 cup yogurt
- 1/3 cup canola oil

INSTRUCTIONS:

1. Preheat the oven to 350°F. Line a muffin pan with cupcake liners.

2. Whisk the milk and vinegar in a measuring cup, and set aside for a few minutes to get good and curdled.

3. Sift the flour, cocoa powder, baking powder, baking soda, and salt into a large bowl, and mix.

4. Place the chocolate chips into a microwave-safe bowl and heat for 30 seconds. Remove from microwave and stir. If they aren't melted, heat again in 10-second increments, stirring each time, until fully melted.

5. In a separate large bowl, mix the curdled milk with the sugar, vanilla extract, yogurt, and oil. Then add the melted chocolate, and mix with a whisk or handheld mixer. Slowly add the dry ingredients a little bit at a time, stopping to scrape the sides of the bowl a few times, and mix until no lumps remain.

6. Fill cupcake liners two-thirds of the way, and bake for 18–22 minutes. Transfer to a cooling rack, and let cool completely before frosting.

Chocolate Frosting

INGREDIENTS:

- 1/4 cup margarine
- 1/4 cup shortening
- 1/2 cup cocoa powder
- 1/2 teaspoon vanilla extract
- 2-1/2 cups confectioners' sugar
- 3 tablespoons milk

INSTRUCTIONS:

1. In a large bowl, with an electric mixer, cream together the margarine and shortening. Sift the cocoa powder into the bowl, and mix with the margarine and shortening.
2. Add the vanilla extract to the mix, and then start beating in the confectioners' sugar in 1/2-cup intervals, adding a little of the milk in between batches. Continue to beat the frosting until it is light and fluffy, about 3–7 minutes.

Reflections

I'm surprised to see Artie standing at the row of sinks when I walk into the girls' bathroom the next morning. "Hey!" She gives me a huge smile and releases her auburn hair, which she had been holding piled on top of her head. It bounces past her shoulders.

"Hi."

She notices me looking at the makeup she has piled on the steel shelf in front of her. "Mom only lets me wear gloss," she explains, motioning to the eyeliner, eye shadow, and mascara. "I keep telling her that everyone wears it, but you know how she is." She shrugs, as if to say, *What choice do I have?*

I don't really know what to say. My mom and I have never discussed makeup, really — mostly because I tried it once and thought it felt slimy. Frankly, I'm just too lazy to wake up extra early and smear a bunch of goop on my face. But I know one thing: If Mom said no, it would never even occur to me to go behind her back and do it anyway. I mean, I might argue with her about it, if it was something I really wanted.

So I'm standing there, wondering if Artie is being brave or not, when she says, "Thanks for leaving those cupcakes last night. They were awesome." She turns back to the mirror and reaches for eyeliner, then opens her mouth wide and squints one eye as she lines the bottom lashes on the other. "Devon thought it was a little weird that you just ducked out without saying good-bye, though."

Three giggling sixth graders push through the bathroom door like toothpaste gushing through a tube. They don't even seem to notice that Artie and I are there as two of them head to the mirror to do their hair and one heads into a stall.

"I didn't want to interrupt your movie."

"That's what I told him." Artie starts applying eyeliner to the other eye. When she finishes, she stands back to survey her work. "Is this even?"

I step up to the mirror and stand beside her, looking at myself and my best friend reflected back at me. Some of the girls in our grade look like they've put on their makeup in the dark, or maybe tried to apply it with a garden trowel — it's either caked on or done in weird colors and looks, in my opinion, horrible.

But Artie looks like a movie star. She's already pretty, but the brown eyeliner brings out the hazel color of her eyes, and the mascara has made her pale lashes seem dark and lush. Her complexion has always been rosy, and the light blush she has applied gives her a pink glow. Her hair is loose around her face, and I'm surprised to realize that my friend isn't just pretty — she's stunning.

Beside her, I feel like I'm fading away, becoming invisible. My wavy hair and bangs seem childish, and my skin is pale after a night lying awake, worrying about the cupcake crisis. I am also, I notice, getting a pimple between my thick, straight eyebrows. I'm thicker than Artie, who seems light and slender in just the right way.

I catch Artie's eye, and she gives me a little half smile, almost as if she feels sorry for me. "Do you want to borrow anything?" she asks, indicating the makeup.

I look at it, momentarily tempted. But I wouldn't know what to do with it. "No, thanks," I say, and she goes back to smearing something on her lips.

The first bell rings, and in a whirl, the giggling sixth graders wash their hands and swirl out the door, leaving me and Artie alone. "Oh, by the way, Hayley, I won't be at lunch today. Devon and I are going to run lines."

This hits me with a chill, and before I know what

I'm doing, I hear myself say, "So — is Devon your boy-friend now?"

Her eyes flick to mine in the mirror. "Why?"

"It's just —" But I've started, and I know that if I don't say anything now, I'll never say anything. And if I never say anything, the distance between us will just grow and grow until we can't reach each other anymore. "I just . . . used to have a crush on him, that's all. So it's a little weird for me."

Artie's eyes flick back to her own reflection. She closes the cap on her lipstick and rubs her lips together. "I know."

For a moment, I'm not sure I've heard her right. My heart is beating double time. "You know that it's weird for me? Or that I had a crush on Devon?"

"Both." Artie drops her makeup into a flowered bag and zips it closed.

"Oh. But you don't care?"

Artie turns to look at me, a condescending smile at the corner of her lips. "What's the big deal, Hayley? You knew that I had a crush on Marco, and it didn't bother you."

"But I didn't — I never meant —" I'm sputtering, as if she's thrown cold water all over me. *I didn't even want him to kiss me! I never asked him to feel that way!*

"So can I help it if Devon likes me, not you?" Artie grabs

her makeup bag and pats me on the shoulder, like I'm a little girl who just lost a sack race. "It's time to grow up, Hayley."

She walks out of the bathroom, leaving me standing there alone.

The homeroom bell rings, but I hardly hear it. I don't cry. For some reason, I can't — instead, I feel nauseated, as if I'll throw up at any minute. I steady myself at the sink, then run some cold water, splashing it on my face, over my mouth.

In the mirror, my eyes look blank.

I feel the way I did when I found out Dad was moving out. *Artie doesn't care about me. Artie cares about Artie, just like Dad cares about Dad.*

It's a lonely thought, and it makes me realize that the little world I'm living in is a place I never really knew, or understood.

Eat Me

I stay in the bathroom for fifteen minutes, skipping home-room altogether. I wouldn't normally do that, but I just can't bear the thought of walking into the room late and having everyone stare at me as I sit down. One year, for Easter, Gran and I poked holes in eggs and blew through them until the yolk and whites spilled into a bowl. That's how I feel right now — emptied, like my insides have been scooped out and scrambled, leaving my outside brittle and fragile.

When the bell rings, signaling the end of homeroom, I step out of the bathroom and join the swarm of students heading to class. I head toward my locker, and just as I am about to reach it, an orange locker door closes and I see Meghan's grinning face.

"Now who on earth would do this for me?" she asks, holding up a cupcake. Taped to the wrapper is a note that reads, EAT ME, I'M GLUTEN FREE! "And how would that person know my locker combination?"

The knot that my guts have been tied in starts to loosen. I even manage a smile. "I don't know — isn't it all prime numbers? Anyone could have guessed that."

"Right." Meghan laughs, creasing the space between her eyebrows. She takes a bite and chews it thoughtfully. "Delicious," she says.

I spin the combination and yank open my locker. "I'm glad you like it."

She looks down at the cupcake. "Nobody's ever done this for me before. I've been to so many birthday parties, and nobody —" She shrugs, takes another bite.

"It wasn't that big a deal."

"Yeah." Meghan dips a finger into the frosting, licks it off the tip. "I guess that's kind of the point."

I don't really know what to say. "So, uh — your mom called my mom last night."

Meghan looks surprised. "Why?"

"Apparently she wants to ban sweets in school. No more cupcakes, no more bake sales —"

"*What?*" Meghan's screech is so loud that a group of eighth-grade girls looks over. Then they put their heads together and start whispering. "Are you serious?"

"Absolutely. You didn't know?"

"Of course not! Gah! If she'd told me, I would've disconnected the phone lines! This is terrible — now everyone is going to think this is because of me."

I don't point out that it kind of *is* because of her.

"*That's* going to make me popular! I'm already borderline with about half of the school because of the Purple Pinto thing," Meghan rants.

"I thought you didn't care what anyone thought about you," I say.

Meghan looks shocked, as if I've just said something crazy. "What gave you that idea?"

"I don't know — the way you dress, the way you just say things . . ."

Meghan considers this for a moment. "I care what people think," she says. "I guess I just usually don't change my mind because of it."

"So — are you going to do something about it?"

"Aside from freak out? I guess I'll have to talk to my mom." Meghan rolls her eyes. "That should be fun."

The second bell's about to ring, so I grab my book and notebook and slam the locker with a clang. "Let me know how it goes."

"I will."

I start to head off, and Meghan calls after me, "Thanks for the cupcake, Hayley!" at the top of her voice.

I laugh, feeling people's eyes on me as I walk down the hall.

This is one case in which I don't mind.

From the Phone Files: Part 3

"Hello?"

"That didn't work."

"What didn't work?"

"Talking to my mom. She gave me one of her standard 'Meghan Markerson, I Am Doing This for Your Own Good and for the Good of the School' lectures."

"So that's no help."

"It's worse than no help — it totally backfired. She's completely dug in. This is my sister's fault."

"How is that possible?"

"Alexis is flunking out of high school. She has this sketchy boyfriend, and she doesn't listen to anything Mom says, so Mom yells at me instead of her."

"Wow."

"It's a fun time around my house lately."

"Yeah. My sister's a little weird, too."

"How so?"

"Oh, I don't know. She has an imaginary friend —"

"I had an imaginary friend until I was ten years old!"

"You did?"

"Yeah. It was a horse."

"Are you serious? Did it . . . talk?"

"Of course not, it was a horse. Anyway, it was a little hard to bring it to school, so I had to invent 'Through Power,' which meant it could go through walls, and stuff."

"So my sister is less weird than you."

"That's what I'm saying!"

Silence.

"So — what should we do about your mom? Just accept our fate?"

"Hayley! What kind of attitude is that? We can't give up now!"

"What are we going to do? Start a petition?"

"Hayley, you're a genius! Of course — that's it! If we show that the whole school is behind us, we'll be able to convince the PTO! I'm hugging you over the phone right now. Can you come over? We've got to plan."

"Why don't you come over here?"

"Sure. Where do you live?"

"Right over the Tea Room."

"That's five blocks from here! I'll be there in twenty minutes."

"See you."

"Bye."

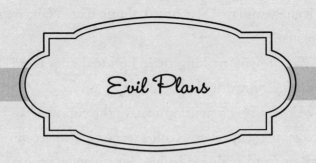

Evil Plans

"What are you girls up to?" Mom looks up from her computer and watches us as we pour ingredients into the gleaming silver commercial mixer. It's enormous — big enough to hold twelve quarts — and Meghan was the one who suggested we use it.

"Gran said we could." I finish pouring in the sugar and turn it on.

"I did," Gran verifies. She rings up a customer as Mom looks from my face to Meghan's, then back again.

She takes a sip of her coffee. "That's fascinating, but it doesn't really answer my question. You just took a batch of cupcakes out of the oven; now you're making more?"

"We're making three hundred chocolate mini-cupcakes to give out at school tomorrow," Meghan explains.

"Gluten free?" Chloe asks.

Meghan smiles. "You heard about that? Nah, these are just regular."

"Why are you making three hundred cupcakes?" Mom asks, one eyebrow lifted.

"We're starting a petition to save the cupcake!"

"Save the cupcake!" Chloe echoes. Rupert mumbles something, and Chloe dissolves into giggles at the end of the counter.

"What is it?" I ask, intrigued by the idea that Rupert might have a sense of humor.

"Are they endangered?" Rupert repeats, more loudly this time.

"Not if I can help it," Meghan says. She tucks a lock of purple hair beneath the hairnet I gave her.

"Isn't that a bribe?" Mom asks.

"Of course not!" Meghan huffs. "It's an incentive! We just want everyone to remember exactly what they'd be giving up."

"And it's good publicity for the Tea Room," I put in.

Gran twinkles, but Mom looks horrified, and I'm about to kick myself: Of course she doesn't want to make enemies out of the PTO! But a moment later, her lips flip down into a thoughtful frown, and she shrugs. "Okay."

The bell over the door jingles, and Mr. Malik bursts in,

smiling. "How am I supposed to sell flowers when my shop smells like chocolate?"

"Would you like a sample?" I ask, holding out a small cupcake. We're on our third batch now. We already frosted the first forty-eight with chocolate and a tiny flower on top.

"Oh! Why, look at this, it's like a tiny tea cake." Mr. Malik accepts the plate I offer him. It's a small plate, but it looks huge with only the tiny cupcake in the center. "Just enough for a single bite."

"They remind me of petit fours," Gran says as she measures Mr. Malik's loose tea into a paper cone.

"Ah, a symbol of a more civilized time," Mr. Malik says as he sits beside my mother at the counter. "A time when people had time!" He looks judgmentally at my mother's computer screen, but she just smiles at him.

"I should make a few for the shop." Gran pours boiling water into the tiny green teapot that's just big enough for her to share with Mr. Malik. "Or perhaps just enough to share."

"Mrs. Wilson, that would be lovely."

My grandmother smiles at Mr. Malik as she holds the teapot lid in place with her hand, then pours out the tea into two china mugs.

"Are these ready to go in?" Meghan asks, gesturing toward the mini-cupcake pan, which I've just filled with batter.

I nod, and she yanks open the commercial oven and pops the tray inside. She closes the door with a *thunk* and looks around the café. "You're so lucky."

"I am?"

"I just love this place." She puts her elbows on the counter and leans her face into her hands. "The light just pours in, and the floor is so wide. I love the plants and the piano."

I look around, taking in the café with new eyes. It's cozy and filled with light, and the wide wooden planks on the floor creak comfortingly whenever you walk across the exact middle of the room. Half of the tables are full. Even Mrs. McTibble is there with her dog, letting her take small bites of her scone. Here and there, vibrant orchids — all from Mr. Malik's store — tower out of their clay pots. The neglected piano stands quietly in the corner. It gets used so rarely that I often forget it's there.

"You should have music here sometimes," Meghan says.

Mom looks up from her computer again, and cocks her head. "What did you say?"

"I said you should have music in here sometimes."

Mom thinks it over. "That might be nice. Maybe for Sunday brunch. A jazz band, or some such."

"You should get the piano tuned," Rupert suggests.

Where is this spurt of conversation coming from? I wonder, as Mom nods and pecks onto her keyboard. "I'll look into it."

"That would be so fun!" Chloe claps her hands. "We could have concerts! Or maybe even a dance performance."

"Don't go crazy," I tell her.

Meghan says, "Why not? The floor is wide enough." She smiles at me, and I can almost hear what she's thinking: *Your sister is* so *not weird.*

The timer chimes, and we pull the cupcakes out of the oven.

They're perfect, and I feel a strange little surge of pride, as if my life is kind of okay, after all.

Nefarious Evildoers

"What's going on here?" Dean Whittier frowns at Meghan, who flashes him an innocent smile.

It's Wednesday, and we're standing near the front entranceway, behind a card table loaded with mini-cupcakes. We've each got a clipboard, which makes us look official. This is something Marco discovered two years ago. He was in a supermarket parking lot, trying to sign up people for a walkathon, but they just kept coming up to him and asking official questions, like, "What are the store hours?" and "Can I have a job application?" He got bored, so he decided to walk around the parking lot, standing in random empty spots, and then — whenever people tried to pull in — telling them that they couldn't park there. He said that nobody argued; they just looked at the clipboard and drove on.

I've always known that story would come in handy someday, and I'm right, because it's only 8:05, and we've already got fifty signatures. Also, I think the cupcakes have been helping. Our table has been mobbed all morning.

Unfortunately, Dean Whittier doesn't seem impressed by the clipboards. "What trouble are you causing now, Ms. Markerson?"

"Do you mean, How am I helping the students express their ideas to the administration?" she corrects him.

"Oh, boy." The dean sighs. "I can already tell I'm going to love this one."

"It has come to our attention" — she points at me, and I resist the urge to duck under the table — "that the PTO plans to ban bake sales and the general presence of sweet treats at school. We simply want to make the students aware of this."

"Look, you're going to have to shut this down."

"Why?"

"You're bribing students with cupcakes."

"We're simply giving away cupcakes. There's no obligation to sign the petition."

I flush as two boys snag cupcakes, then dart away from the table. "Those guys didn't sign," I point out.

"Would you like a cupcake, Dean Whittier?" Meghan asks.

"No, thank you. I'm not sure that's appropriate."

"Would you like to sign the petition?" I ask.

Dean Whittier looks at me in surprise, then laughs. "I'm not sure that's appropriate, either."

"Nice try, though, right?" Meghan says with a grin. "Hayley's good."

"Don't let her get you into too much mischief, Ms. Hicks," the dean says, and walks away. I'm shocked that he knows my name, and wonder if it's a good sign or a bad one.

"Nice one!" Meghan holds her palm up for a high five, and I slap it.

Once the dean is gone, the traffic at our table picks up. Almost everybody is furious to hear that the PTO wants to ban sweets. One kid even threatens to sue the school if the measure passes. That's Omar Gomez, though, whose mother is a lawyer. He's basically always threatening to sue somebody.

I catch sight of Ezra, and call him over. "Sign this petition," I tell him, thrusting my clipboard at him.

He frowns, but takes a cupcake, anyway. "What's up?"

"The PTO wants to ban cupcakes, bake sales, you name it."

"What? That's how we raise money for our soccer uniforms!"

"Not anymore, if you don't sign this petition."

Ezra signs, and immediately calls over his teammate Tom Stacco, who calls over Evangeline Jackson, the captain of the girls' soccer team. Soon we have members from both teams helping us, handing out cupcakes and asking for signatures, and before I know it, I'm face-to-face with Marco.

"Hi," I say.

His eyes are flat and hard. "You have a petition?"

"Yeah." I get the clipboard back from an eighth-grade girl and hand it to Marco. "It's really great that you're signing this." I know my voice sounds gushy, but I can't help it. I wish he would just look at me and smile, let me know that things are okay between us.

He looks up at me with that same flat expression, almost as if I'm not even there. "I signed it for the soccer team, not for you, Hayley."

I try hard not to flinch, though my face stings as if I've been slapped. He starts to turn away, but before his eyes fully leave mine, I hear myself ask, "Would you like a cupcake?"

Marco stares at me for a long moment, long enough for another person from the soccer team to grab the clipboard out of my hand. Then he takes a cupcake and walks away, slowly pulling the paper wrapper from the side.

Someone puts the clipboard back into my hand just in time for Kyle to ask if he can sign. I give him the clipboard without thinking, until finally he has to ask me where he should put his name.

"Oh! I'm so sorry, Kyle. Here." I take his hand and guide it halfway down the page.

"Hayley! We're out of cupcakes," Meghan says.

"Are you kidding?"

"I'm scratching out my name," Kyle announces.

"No! Don't. I'll make you a cupcake," I promise.

Kyle grins, revealing a dimple in his right cheek. "I was just kidding."

"Oh."

"But I'll take that cupcake."

"Okay. I don't know when I'll have time —"

"Anytime," he says, and in the next moment, someone pushes him aside and grabs the clipboard from me (again) just as the first bell rings.

The students around our table scatter like minnows surprised by a stone splashing into their pond. I help Meghan fold up the table. "I've got it," she says. "Mrs. Diamond said I can store it in the office."

"Are you sure?"

"It's light! See you in homeroom."

I grin at her, then notice a familiar auburn head bobbing down the hall. Seeing a chance for one more signature, I sprint after her. "Artie!" I shout. "Hey! Wait up!"

She turns around and looks at me, her eyebrows lifted in surprise. "Hi, Hayley."

"Um, listen, would you sign this petition?" I briefly explain about the PTO, then hand Artie a pen.

To my surprise, she doesn't reach for the clipboard.

"What's up?" I ask.

"You're starting a petition?"

"Meghan and I are, yeah."

Artie's eyes narrow, but she nods, as if that's the information she was expecting. "I should have known."

"What does *that* mean?"

"I don't know. . . . Isn't this just a little . . . juvenile?"

My heart is thudding in my chest. Juvenile? *Juvenile?* My mouth falls open, but the words are still frozen on my lips. I feel as if I'm made of sand, about to blow away in the wind. "Artie, I —"

She purses her lips. "Look, Hayley, I've been meaning to talk to you. I don't want to be called Artie anymore."

"What? What should I call you?"

Seriously, I'm expecting her to say Fabulosa, or Queen Janice, or something equally weird, but what she says is, "My name is Artemis. Devon says that someone with a name as beautiful as that shouldn't have a boy's nickname."

"But — but —" The bell rings, and Artie — Artemis — frowns.

"I'm late. I'll see you, okay?" And she gives me a friendly little pat on the shoulder — the kind of thing you might do to a child or a dog — and dashes off to her locker.

I stare after her for a moment, wondering who on earth she is.

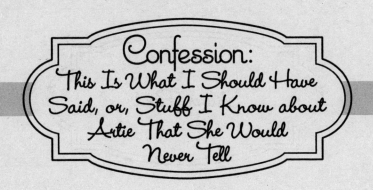

Confession: This Is What I Should Have Said, or, Stuff I Know about Artie That She Would Never Tell

Juvenile? Juvenile is when you call the radio show fifteen times to request that they play the *Batman* theme song!

Juvenile is when you sing to your cat! Juvenile is when you dare your best friend to eat a worm!

Juvenile is when you hide your Barbies under the bed so you can still play with them — even during your first year in middle school!

Juvenile is when you put your finger into the pencil sharpener to see what happens!

Juvenile is when you write a fan letter to the Muppets!

Juvenile is when you tell your best friend not to use the name she's been calling you since you were both two years old!

That's juvenile.

That's what's juvenile, okay?

Silver Bird

A million more responses to the word *juvenile* are bubbling in my mind as I yank open the door to the drugstore and storm down the school supplies aisle. Meghan has asked me to pick up some poster board and make a couple of signs to take to the PTO meeting. Of course I said yes. It's the least I can do — after all, she's going to be making the presentation. I'll just stand back and hold up my CUPCAKES ARE NOT A CRIME sign.

Anyway, so I'm just standing there, trying to decide between neon pink and neon green, when who should come around the aisle holding a bottle of shampoo but Annie.

She lets out a startled "Oh!" then smiles, and then looks down at the shampoo in her hand as if she wants to make sure it isn't anything embarrassing.

"Hi," I say.

"Hello." We both stand there awkwardly, and I wonder if she wants to run away as badly as I do. Instead, we're held there by some weird force of politeness, and it's clear that neither one of us will escape until we think of something to say to each other.

"Getting shampoo?" I know — how did I think up something so brilliant, right?

"For some reason, I've had the same bottle of conditioner for two years, but I keep running out of shampoo." I look at her long, lustrous black hair and can't believe she doesn't even need conditioner.

She notices the neon poster board in my hand. "Project?"

"Extracurricular," I explain. "The school wants to ban cupcakes."

She looks bemused. "Why?"

"Childhood obesity, food allergies, and concerns about safe food preparation."

"Oh. Those are good reasons." She shrugs.

"But I think people should be allowed to choose what they eat."

"Well, it isn't like you go to a school full of small children, right?"

"No — the youngest are eleven, the oldest thirteen. Some are fourteen."

Annie laughs. "I could cook dinner and take care of my baby sister when I was eight! How are you going to tell people who are almost adults what to do?"

"Exactly."

A smile still plays at the edges of Annie's lips. "My mouth still waters when I think about that cupcake you made the other day. It would be" — she searches for a word — "unfortunate . . . if your schoolmates couldn't share in your passion."

Share in my passion? I never really thought of cupcakes as a passion before, but I guess she's right. And when she puts it that way, it doesn't sound juvenile at all. "Thank you," I say.

Annie nods, then seems to think of something. "When will they decide?"

"There's a meeting tonight," I explain.

She places her shampoo carefully on a shelf of notebooks, then reaches behind her neck to unclasp the delicate bird necklace she's wearing. She holds it out to me. "My mother gave me this when I was your age," she explains. "It's good luck."

I hold up a hand, palm out. "I can't." I couldn't possibly take something that special.

Annie's face falls. I quickly say, "Maybe I could just borrow it."

She smiles and steps behind me, and I hold up my hair as she fastens the clasp. The bird is light against my neck. "I feel luckier already," I tell her.

I expect a laugh, but instead, she cocks her head thoughtfully. "Of course, it is sometimes hard to recognize luck. Often things that appear lucky turn out to be unlucky. And sometimes things that appear unlucky are really good luck in disguise. It all depends on the angle from which you see it."

"I guess."

She smiles at me, then picks up her shampoo bottle. We say good-bye. I don't want to have to stand next to her in line, so I pretend like I'm still trying to decide which poster board to buy and stand in front of the school supplies for another five minutes, staring blankly and thinking about what she said. Like, running into Annie at the drugstore seemed unlucky at first. But she seemed to understand the cupcake cause — and she loaned me her lucky necklace.

And having Meghan's mother want to ban the cupcakes seemed unlucky, but it gave me a chance to get to know Meghan better. So maybe it was lucky.

Chloe lost her friends . . . but now she's friends with Rupert. Is that lucky?

I guess it's hard to know.

Something Mysterious

"Hey, Gran."

My grandmother looks up from what she's doing, which is . . . something mysterious. A tiny piece of cake is suspended on the end of a fork, and she's pouring some thick pink liquid over it.

"You're just in time to learn to make petit fours!" Gran grins at me, delighted.

"I've already tried one," Mom says from her usual place at the end of the counter. "They're delicious."

"Cool." I stow my bag and poster board beneath the counter and go wash my hands. "Are we getting the piano fixed?" I gesture to the workman hovering over the old upright.

"Tuned," Mom corrects. "I don't think it's been tuned in —"

"Thirteen years!" Gran chirps. She places a hand to the

side of her lips and whispers to me, "Honestly, I practically forgot the thing was sitting there."

"So what's this stuff?" I ask, pointing to the vaguely icing-like goo.

"Fondant," Gran explains. "Let me show you." With a deft hand, she uses a small cookie cutter to slice out a square of sponge cake. When she lifts it out, I see that it's actually two layers of cake with raspberry jam in the middle. Then she places the tiny cake on the fork and ladles the pink fondant over it. "Now we let this dry, and we can decorate it with tiny flowers."

"They look more like candies than cakes."

"Fairy-sized treats," Gran says, and I am flush with a vivid memory — making a fairy house in the woods with Gran and leaving a small cake for them. Pink icing, a tiny red flower on top.

"Have we made these before?"

"Oh, once or twice, perhaps. When you were a small girl."

I try my hand at the fondant — it doesn't come out as evenly as Gran's — and reach for another small square of cake. Mom watches me for a moment. "Is that a new necklace?"

"Dang!" I've dropped the cake into the fondant. Gran hands me a spoon, and I fish it out. "Now it's a blob."

"It's all right, darling, just try again." Gran hands me another piece.

"Where did you get it?" Mom asks. She's still talking about the necklace.

I feel a two-second temptation to lie, but reject the idea. "Annie gave it to me."

"Annie?" Mom cocks her head.

"Dad's new . . . friend." *Ugh.* The word tastes foul in my mouth.

"Ah." Mom turns back to her computer, and I feel Gran's sideways glance at me. Luckily, Mrs. McTibble comes in at just that moment, grouching about the weather, and Gran bustles off to help her — or at least commiserate with her, which is more or less the same thing.

Mom and I are at the far end of the counter. I'm really, really focusing on pouring fondant on the petit four I'm making. Out of the blue, Mom says, "Do you like Annie?"

I don't look up from my work. "I don't hate Annie," I reply.

Mom nods. "It's okay if you like her."

"Okay." I place the petit four on a rack to dry. "But I'm not sure if I do."

Mom presses her lips together, and I can tell she's trying not to laugh. "It's nice she gave you that necklace."

"She's trying, I guess. Maybe too hard."

"That's understandable. She's in an awkward position."

I look into my mom's warm brown eyes. "It doesn't upset you to talk about her?"

"No, honey." Mom shakes her head slowly, our eyes still locked. "People have to move on. We're at a new place in our lives now. Things aren't going back."

For some reason, I feel my throat tighten, like something's stuck in it, and my eyes burn. Just then, the piano tuner comes over to talk to Mom, and I surreptitiously swipe at my eyes. She writes him a check as Rupert and Chloe walk into the café.

"Oh, it's tuned!" Rupert says when he sees the workman's bag on the floor. "May I play something?" He's asking me, which is hilarious, because I have no idea — it's not like I'm in charge.

"Customers don't want to hear banging on an old piano," Mrs. McTibble grumbles, but Gran says, "Certainly, dear," and settles Mrs. McTibble with a look.

I'm about to tell Gran that maybe it's not a good idea — after all, we do have a couple of customers, and Mrs. McTibble just might be right. But then Mom's phone rings, and when she sees who it's from, she gives a little "Oh" of surprise and flashes me a look I can't read. I watch her dash into the back to answer the call, and when I turn around Rupert is already sitting down at the piano bench. His fingers pause over the keys, as if he's trying to remember something. Then an expression comes over his face like the look Marco gets when he's thinking hard, and Rupert launches into playing the piano.

His fingers fly over the keys, rising and falling as the notes fill the café. They're like birds, swooping and diving through the air, and the next thing I know, Chloe has begun to dance. She's wearing a spring dress, and her skirt swirls around her as she twists and twirls her body.

My sister has always taken ballet, and her movements are graceful and fluid, but different from anything I've ever seen her do before. There is an open area at the rear of the café, and she fills it with her dancing the way that Rupert fills it with music. For both of them, it's as if they've forgotten that the rest of us are here, or they don't care.

Mrs. McTibble sits back in her seat, and Gwendolyn falls asleep in her arms, letting out a soft, happy snore. Gran props her elbows on the counter and watches, and someone opens the door to enter, but pauses in the doorway, unwilling to disturb the scene.

After a few moments, Rupert's music slows, and the final chord sounds. Chloe comes to a graceful rest as the notes die away, and for a moment, silence reverberates in the café.

"Well," Gran says finally. "That was lovely. Thank you, Rupert. And Chloe, you too."

Rupert smiles shyly and Chloe curtsies. The customer in the doorway takes a step forward, and in the next moment, the spell is broken. We're back in a café. But something has shifted.

Rupert has changed in my eyes. And so has Chloe. I feel as if I'm waking from a dream in which I felt sorry for Chloe for having a strange little companion instead of her old friends. Now I see that those friends were just like . . . like old shoes. Even if you still want to wear them, they don't fit anymore.

Rupert fits.

I'm still mulling this over when Mom comes out of the back office, her face pale.

"Are you okay?" Chloe asks.

"Yes." Mom looks down at the phone.

"Who was that?"

"It was Mr. Alper from Greater Valley Family Practice. The doctors' office."

"Oh."

"He offered me the job."

"Even though you snorted water through your nose?" I ask as Chloe lets out a whoop and twirls around our mother.

"I guess he thought that was funny." Mom looks down at the phone, as if she can't believe she just had that conversation.

"That's great!" I rush over to give my mom a hug, and it's only when I finish squeezing her that I turn around and see Gran watching us, a faint, sad smile on her face.

"Well. Congratulations, Margaret. He's lucky to have you."

"Thanks, Mother."

And I see in her hesitant face that Mom isn't sure this is the right thing. Even though it's what she wanted — what we all wanted. Now she can earn enough money to save up and move out of Gran's. She won't have to manage the café anymore.

But.

But then we'll move out of Gran's.

"When do you start?" I ask.

"I told them I'd have to think about it."

"You did?" And the rush of relief that floods my body is a surprise, even to me. I hug her again, more tightly this time.

"Why?" Chloe asks.

"I just want to be sure it's the right thing before I make any decisions."

I want my mother to do what she wants. Of course. She needs to be happy. But I can't stand to think about leaving Gran's house. Not yet.

I know it's selfish . . . but I guess I just don't want anything else to change right now.

Freak-outs

(makes approximately 12 cupcakes)

Try these when you're feeling freaked, or just in the mood for something different. Very, very different.

INGREDIENTS:

    8 whole cloves garlic

    1/3 cup canola oil, plus more to coat garlic

    1 cup milk

    1 teaspoon apple cider vinegar

    1 cup plus 2 tablespoons all-purpose flour

    1 teaspoon baking powder

    1/2 teaspoon baking soda

    1/2 teaspoon salt

    3/4 cup sugar

    1-1/2 teaspoons vanilla extract

    2/3 cup semisweet chocolate chips

    kosher salt, for sprinkling

INSTRUCTIONS:

1. Preheat the oven to 350°F. Line a muffin pan with cupcake liners.
2. Toss garlic cloves in a little oil and place on a

baking sheet. Roast in the oven until browned and soft. Remove from oven, and let sit until cool enough to mash into a paste.

3. Whisk the milk and vinegar in a bowl, and set aside for a few minutes to get good and curdled.

4. Sift the flour, baking powder, baking soda, and salt into a large bowl, and mix.

5. Place the chocolate chips in a microwave-safe bowl and heat for 30 seconds. Remove from microwave and stir. If they aren't melted, heat again in 10-second increments, stirring each time, until fully melted.

6. In a separate large bowl, mix the curdled milk with the sugar, vanilla extract, and oil, then add the garlic paste and melted chocolate. With a whisk or handheld mixer, add the dry ingredients a little bit at a time, stopping occasionally to scrape the sides of the bowl, and mix until no lumps remain.

7. Fill cupcake liners two-thirds of the way, and bake for 18–22 minutes. Transfer to a cooling rack, and let cool completely before frosting. Frost with Fudgy Frosting, and then sprinkle a few flakes of kosher salt on top.

Fudgy Frosting

INGREDIENTS:

   1/3 cup semisweet chocolate chips

   1/2 cup margarine, softened

   2 teaspoons vanilla extract

   3 tablespoons cocoa powder, unsweetened

   1/2 cup powdered milk (non-flavored, otherwise the texture will be grainy from the larger sugar crystals)

   1 cup confectioners' sugar

   1 tablespoon milk (to thin frosting, if needed)

INSTRUCTIONS:

1. Place the chocolate chips into a microwave-safe bowl and heat for 30 seconds. Remove from microwave and stir. If they aren't melted, heat again in 10-second increments, stirring each time, until fully melted. Then set aside and allow to cool to room temperature.

2. In a large bowl, with an electric mixer, beat the margarine until light and fluffy. Beat in vanilla extract and cocoa powder until combined.

3. Slowly beat in the powdered milk and

confectioners' sugar on low speed. If the mixture seems too firm, drizzle in a little milk; if it's too watery, add more powdered milk in small increments. Beat on medium speed until completely combined.

Still Freaking Out!

"Are you nervous?" Mom asks as we walk toward the upstairs conference room, where the meeting is to be held.

"A little." I don't want to admit that I'm nervous just *walking* there — I've never been in that room before. "I'm just glad I don't have to do the talking."

"Meghan's going to give the presentation?"

"Yes." *Thank goodness*, I add silently. In third grade, I flunked an oral report on *Bambi*. When I got to the part about Bambi's mother dying, I started to cry, and then I had to sit down, and my teacher gave me an F.

I've hated oral reports ever since.

"Speak of the devil," Mom says — Meghan is standing in the hallway. When she sees me, she darts over and takes my arm.

"Are you okay?" I ask her. Her eyes and the tip of her nose are red.

"I'm going inside," Mom says, reading Meghan's face.

I nod and turn back to my friend. "What's wrong?"

"I just had a huge fight with my mom," she whispers. "She's freaking out that I'm trying to stop her."

"Ohmigosh." I don't know what to do, so I give her a big hug, which is pretty awkward, given that I'm holding a huge sign. A few people gape at us as they walk into the meeting.

Meghan puts her palms to her cheeks, as if she's trying to stop them from burning. "You've got to help me," she says.

"Anything."

"You've got to give the presentation."

"Anything else."

"I mean it, Hayley. I can't do it!" She pulls a pile of index cards from her jacket pocket. Her hands are shaking, and I feel her fear. This is a side of Meghan that I've never witnessed before — she always seems so confident, so happy. It's strange to think that she's afraid of her own mother, but I can see the desperation in her eyes when she begs, "I wouldn't ask you if it wasn't important."

Her fear transfers to me, almost like a blood transfusion. Suddenly, I'm sweating and my breath is shallow. I can't do this! I'm the sidekick — the person holding the sign, not the person making the speech! "Meghan — you're the one who's good at this stuff!" Her face reddens and her eyes fill, and I'm feeling horrible, but still I blurt out, "I can't do it."

She turns a darker shade of red. "You have to." Meghan's stare presses down on me and I feel small. "You've done harder stuff than this, Hayley." Her voice is like the crack of a whip, and I almost shrink away from her. Meghan's angry, and I don't really blame her. But her voice changes suddenly, and she's almost pleading. "I'm asking you as a friend to do me this favor."

The word sinks into me. As a friend? I blow out a sigh. This is a Meghan I barely know — frightened, almost needy — and for a moment I wish that I'd never put that cupcake in her locker. "Okay," I say finally.

"Okay, like, you'll do it?" Her face is cautiously hopeful, and I realize suddenly that she wasn't sure I'd say yes. But of course I'm saying yes. Didn't she help me when I couldn't remember my locker combination? Didn't she help me when I saw Devon with Artie?

"I'll do it."

She hugs me, hard.

"Don't squish the sign!"

"Of course not." Meghan takes the poster right out of my hand. "I have to hold it, don't I?" She grins, and wipes her face with her sleeve. "Do I look horrible?"

"You look great."

Meghan rolls her eyes. Then she fluffs out her purple bangs and straightens her hot-pink tunic. She takes a deep breath and reaches for my hand.

"Just remember," I tell her.

"What?"

"Nineteen, twenty-three, twenty-nine."

She doesn't exactly laugh, but she lets out a little huff — an almost chuckle — and I know she understands what I mean. Then she smiles at me and sniffs through her pink nose, and we walk into the meeting together.

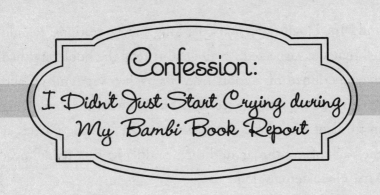

Confession: I Didn't Just Start Crying during My Bambi Book Report

ctually, I threw up.

It was because I hadn't really read the book. I saw the Walt Disney movie, and decided I would try to bluff my way through the report. I don't know why I decided to do that. I had never done it before.

I'd had a cheeseburger for lunch, and it sat heavy in my stomach during math, while I was waiting for language arts to start, and my oral book report to begin. I guess I was loaded down with guilt, and I was dreading getting up before the class.

And when I did, Ellen Criswell was sitting in the front row. She and I had always been friendly, and she flashed a goofy face at me as I started. I guess she could tell I was nervous.

Anyway, so I described the opening of the book (movie),

and Mrs. Hochstetter started asking a few questions. I could tell that she suspected I really hadn't read the book, and had maybe cribbed my report from its back cover (guilty), and her questions made me feel sick. She knew I was lying! Lying in front of the whole class! I stood there, tasting pickles at the back of my throat, and then, suddenly, I barfed all over Mrs. Hochstetter's desk.

Then Ellen barfed, too.

I think it was the smell.

Ellen and I had to go to the nurse, while everyone else went to recess so the janitor could clean up.

I got a D on my report, but I was too afraid to show it to my mother, so I never got it signed. And in Mrs. Hochstetter's class, that meant that your grade automatically went down an entire letter. To an F.

I worked like crazy for the rest of the semester and managed to pull my language arts grade up to a B. But I still can't eat a cheeseburger or think about Bambi without feeling queasy.

And oral reports?

Barf city.

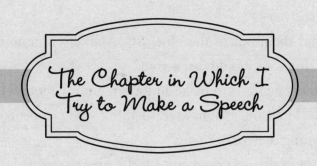

The Chapter in Which I
Try to Make a Speech

The meeting starts with a lot of boring talk about the meeting the month before. Someone wants to make a change in the minutes, and everyone has to talk it over before they can finally agree.

The members of the PTO are all seated around a long oval table. I see my mom sitting near one end. Beside her is a blond woman with large teeth, and I can tell by the nervous glances Meghan keeps flashing at her that it's her mother.

I'm barely paying attention as Ms. Markerson launches into the cupcake issue, and her reasons for wanting to keep sweets off the streets. Instead, I'm cataloging everything I had for dinner — rice-and-bean burrito, spinach salad, raspberry cupcake — and trying not to picture it spewed across the conference table.

I will not throw up.

I will not —

And then, out of the blue, Ms. Markerson announces, "So I think we should cast a vote."

Someone starts to make a motion, but my mother interrupts. "Hold on," Mom says. "I think some students have something they want to say."

And in the next moment, I feel everyone staring at me.

Meghan thrusts her note cards into my hand, and I can taste the burrito. I swallow hard as I stand on my wobbly feet. "Uh, yeah," I say as I look down at the cards. "Um, we wanted to . . ." But my vision blurs, my head feels light. Meghan's notes aren't making any sense to me.

I glance at Meghan, who is smiling at me in a way that is supposed to seem encouraging, but actually comes off as a grimace of terror. The words on the note card swim together. I have the same horrible feeling I had in Mrs. Hochstetter's class. . . .

"Is this really necessary?" asks a bald man at the end of the table. "It doesn't seem that there's any need to discuss cupcakes. This is a health and public safety issue."

"I think we should hear the students out." My mother's voice is calm, strong. Her office voice.

But the bald man just huffs. "Listening to children who want to eat sugar just seems a little juvenile."

The PTO laughs, but the word *juvenile* splashes over me like a bucket of ice water. My mind clears. I straighten up. "No," I hear myself say. "It isn't juvenile. Not at all."

Someone chuckles, and I plant my feet firmly on the ground. I feel everyone staring, and stutter, "Th-the sports teams —"

"Would you speak up a little?" A sharp-featured woman leans forward in her chair.

I lick my dry lips and start again. "The sports teams use bake sales to raise money for uniforms —"

"They can hold a walkathon." The bald man waves his hand dismissively, and others around the table nod. "That way they would be encouraging a healthy lifestyle."

"But our sports teams are already encouraging exercise. Besides, a walkathon and a bake sale aren't the same thing," I counter. "At a bake sale, you're making something and selling it. At a walkathon, you're just asking for donations." I put the cards on my chair. "But that doesn't matter. What we're talking about here is individual liberty, and the ability to make choices. The students at Adams Middle School aren't small children, or people who need protection from poor nutrition. We're old enough to decide what we eat, and how much. We pack our own lunches. We choose what we want from the cafeteria. You have to decide how much you can trust us. Can you trust us enough to let us eat a cupcake once in a while?"

The room is quiet as I take the cards from my chair and sit down. I look over at Meghan, who is beaming at me like a proud mother. She takes my hand and squeezes the life out of it. I feel light-headed and shaky, but my mom smiles at me from across the room, and I realize that the two people I care about think I did a good job. That's something.

"Thank you." Meghan's mother nods at me and smiles at me with her big teeth. "Now, I'd like to put the matter before the PTO. I have here" — she holds up a piece of paper — "a proposal to ban the sale and distribution of sweet treats at Adams Middle School."

"So — the students could still bring a treat in their lunch?" This is from the sharp-featured woman.

Ms. Markerson hesitates. "Yes," she says. "We simply won't allow treats to be handed out to the whole class or sold. All those in favor?" And before I know what's happening, five members of the PTO put up their hands and say aye.

Ms. Markerson asks for those against, and my mother and two others say nay, and just like that, the vote is over and we've lost.

Loserville

We have to sit through a bunch of other blah blah blah before Meghan's mother finally wraps up the meeting and the PTO files out. Meghan's mother pauses as she passes us, but in the end, she doesn't say anything. She just walks out.

I keep my eyes on my lap. I can't look up. I feel the heaviness of my failure sticking to me, like rain weighting my clothes.

Meghan has been holding my hand this whole time, but she finally drops it. "Well . . . that was horrible," she says, her voice almost a whisper.

"I'm so sorry."

"You're sorry?"

I nod, then feel her touch my sleeve.

"Hayley, you were great. Great! Your speech was way better than what I had written. You were perfect! This is crazy!"

I look over at her, and see the earnestness in her face. Her jaw is set, her face pale. "My mother had the votes before we even came in here."

"She did?"

"I could tell." Meghan's voice trembles a little, and I realize how powerless she feels.

"It's okay."

"You were great," she says again. "Better than I could have done it."

This isn't true, but it seems lame to disagree with her. I wish I knew what to say to her about her mother. I wish I understood why her mother needed to make a big deal out of cupcakes — why she couldn't just let Meghan deal with the situation her own way. "Sometimes people make no sense." It's the only thing I can think of.

Meghan looks at me. "They always make sense," she says. "It's just that sometimes they aren't who you thought they were."

I think about my dad, and about Artie. I think about Marco, too. None of them are the people I thought they were. Maybe they've changed and maybe they haven't. But now that I see them from a new angle, I guess I can't go back to seeing them the way I did before.

My mother pokes her head in through the door, giving us a sympathetic smile. "Girls, can I interest you in a cupcake?"

"Is it gluten free?" Meghan asks.

"We still have a couple of those left," I say, but Meghan shakes her head.

"I was actually just kidding. I have to go home." Meghan's voice is like lead. She casts a glance toward the hallway, where her mother is chatting with a couple of PTO members. We walk to the door and Meghan slowly goes over and stands beside her mother, as quiet as a shadow.

I feel shaky, almost as if I've discovered a secret about Meghan, as I follow Mom downstairs. We walk through the eerily quiet school and out into the night.

"You were wonderful," Mom says. I can hear our footsteps as we head to the car. Above, the stars are dim, tiny points compared to the stars I saw at Alex's party. I know it's because of the light pollution — we're closer to town, with all of its streetlamps and houses and large-screen TVs — but it feels like the world is just dimmer.

"Not good enough."

"I think you made a few people in there think. And you did what was important to you."

I know that this is supposed to be a pep talk, but it isn't really having much of an effect. "I guess."

We come to the car, which chirps as Mom unlocks it. We slip into our seats and click our seat belts closed, but Mom doesn't put her key in the ignition. Instead, she says, "You were really brave, Hayley."

We are both staring straight ahead, through the windshield and into the dark night. "Thanks, Mom."

"You made me want to be brave."

"You *are* brave, Mom."

We look at each other a moment. Her features are indistinct in the dim light. I feel like I am about to cry. Why? Because of the cupcakes? Because I let Meghan down?

"Hayley, what if I told you that I didn't want to work at Greater Valley Family Practice?"

"What?"

Mom sighs. "I don't want that job, Hayley. I think . . . I think I want to work at the café. Help Mother run it."

I'm quiet for a moment, taking this in.

"Would you think I was crazy?" Mom asks.

"No. I'd think you were sane."

"Really?"

I smile. It's funny to hear Mom treating me like I'm the adult, and I think she realizes it at the same time I do, because she laughs.

"You have to help Gran with the café," I say. "You're so good at it."

Mom holds out her arms, and I lean in for a hug. Mom is

soft and the very best hug-giver in the world. "I'm so proud of you, honey," she says.

"Same here."

We drive home in comfortable silence, both lost in our thoughts, and Mom pulls into a parking spot halfway up the street from the Tea Room.

"What's going on?" Mom asks, and I see as soon as she does that two police officers are standing outside the door of the café. A face appears in the window, and a moment later, Chloe bounds out through the door. "Thank goodness you're here! We need your help!"

Mom and I both rush over. "What's wrong?" Mom asks, and I can tell from her voice that her heart is pounding as fast as mine.

"Wrong?" Chloe looks at her, then shakes her head. "Mom! The place is packed!"

And then we see that the police officers are simply standing in the line, waiting to be served. The Tea Room is jammed — every table is taken. The air is alive with noise — people chatting, china clinking, and a piano playing.

"Rupert has been at it for half an hour," Chloe says over her shoulder as we follow her inside.

Mom and I hurry to wash our hands and put on aprons. Gran is serving at the counter, beaming at the young police officers. When I look around, I recognize several faces from school. Even Marco is here. He notices me and gives a half wave, then turns to his friends.

I wave back. "What's going on?" I ask Chloe.

"No clue," my sister says. "I'll bus the tables, you ring the register. Gran is busy charming the customers."

Mom is already brewing a fresh pot of coffee, so I follow orders and take the register. I ring up five orders and the next person is Kyle, who's standing with three of his friends. "Hey, Kyle," I say. "It's Hayley," I add, since it's loud and I'm not sure he can hear me very well.

"I figured," Kyle says with a grin. "What's up? Sounds pretty crowded."

"Yeah, like, half the school is here."

"I guess everyone liked that cupcake giveaway," Kyle says, and the words crash over me suddenly.

"Oh! The cupcake giveaway." I'd forgotten about it. Suddenly, Marco being here means something to me. He's supporting my cupcake fight. And so are the other kids. I feel a rush of gratitude, but I can't help noticing who isn't here: Artie.

"How did that work out, by the way? The petition, I mean."

"We lost."

"Too bad. You fought the good fight, Hayley."

"Thanks."

"So — what's the cupcake du jour?"

"It's lemon with white-chocolate frosting," I say.

"Sounds great. What are you calling it?"

I think about it for a moment. "It's a Good Fight cup-cake," I decide on the spot.

Kyle smiles at me. "Don't you owe me one?" he says.

"Oh! Right. I forgot." I place one on a plate and hand it over. "On the house."

"I was just kidding, Hayley. I'll pay for it." He reaches into his pocket.

"Forget it, Kyle."

"You sure?" His smile is radiant.

"Absolutely."

"And that, Hayley Hicks, is why you are the coolest girl at Adams."

I blush a little, but decide to let the compliment sink in. The coolest girl at Adams?

Well, who am I to disagree?

Just like everything, I guess it just depends on the angle from which you see it.

Kailyn
Wong

Acknowledgments

I would like to gratefully acknowledge the help of my sister, Zoë Papademetriou, who created the recipes in this book. I would also like to thank my editor Anamika Bhatnagar for her insight and input, my agent Rosemary Stimola for her unwavering enthusiasm, my husband for his willingness to listen to all of my thoughts and ideas, and my mother for her relentless support.

Don't miss Hayley's latest confessions!

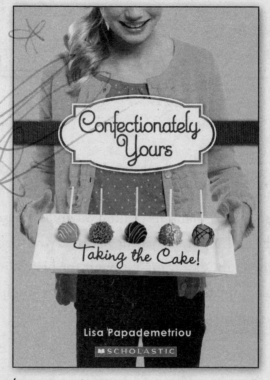

Hayley and Artie aren't totally clicking these days — and they're definitely no longer best friends. To top it off, Hayley's still crushing on someone who might just be Artie's new boyfriend. This mess really takes the cake!